A Clash of Class

BY BERNARD C. BARTON

Note for Librarians: A cataloguing record for this book is available from Library and Archives Canada at www.collectionscanada.ca/amicus/index-e.html

Printed in Victoria, BC, Canada.

ISBN: 978-1-4269-0978-8 (sc)

Our mission is to efficiently provide the world's finest, most comprehensive book publishing service, enabling every author to experience success. To find out how to publish your book, your way, and have it available worldwide, visit us online at www.trafford.com

Trafford rev. 8/12/2009

North America & international
toll-free: 1 888 232 4444 (USA & Canada)
phone: 250 383 6864 ♦ fax: 812 355 4082

Riches and honor are with me.
Proverbs 8:18

Part I.

JEROME AND REBECCA: FIRST LOVE

O N A cool evening in mid February, Jerome Callaghan walked to the home of his close friend, Alan Cranwell. The two of them had enjoyed this friendship since primary school days. This evening Alan wanted to introduce his cousin, Rebecca, to Jerome.

"I think the two of you will get on well together," Alan had told Jerome.

"Didn't you say she is just fifteen?" replied Jerome.

"Yes, but she's very mature."

"Fifteen, and very mature. Hmm," mused Jerome," that's almost a contradiction."

Jerome was the last to arrive for the Cranwell's annual Valentine's party. Inside reverberated with the noisy chatter of some eighteen young people enjoying the party. Jeanette, Alan's young sister, greeted Jerome at the front door with her typical enthusiasm, and hugged him warmly.

"Jerome, it's good to see you. I'm so glad you could come."

"I wouldn't miss a party at the Cranwell's," Jerome responded with a broad smile.

"Now let me introduce you to Rebecca," said Jeanette eagerly.

"Oh yes, that's my real purpose for being here, isn't it?" Jerome chuckled.

"Jerome, you're teasing," quipped Jeanette. "Tonight your life will change," she announced with a theatrical flourish.

Jerome was surprised. Rebecca was tall, and could easily pass for eighteen. Her short auburn hair was exquisitely shaped, and she held Jerome's attention with her dark blue eyes and warm smile. Hardly your usual fifteen-year-old, thought Jerome, as Jeanette introduced her cousin.

"Hello Jerome," said Rebecca in a soft, clear voice. There was no embarrassed giggle that so often accompanied such introductions. She possessed poise unusual in someone her age.

"Alan tells me you're writing your Higher School Cert exams in June, and you're hoping to win a scholarship to Cambridge," continued Rebecca.

"Well, Rebecca, you don't bother with first meeting trivia," said a rather surprised Jerome.

"Oh, would you rather I did? You know. Where do you live? Have you lived there long? What school do you go to? Alan told me all that long ago. It's just that he's taken longer than expected to arrange this meeting." Rebecca was smiling at Jerome.

"Now that you know everything about me, I presume I may begin interrogating you."

"Not exactly," said Rebecca, still smiling, "but you may ask questions."

"It's becoming clear, you're a lawyer's daughter." Jerome was smiling appreciatively.

"You don't do so badly yourself. Joking aside, Alan is very impressed with your academic achievements. As far as he's concerned, your scholarship is a 'fait accompli.'"

"After my mother, Alan is my staunchest fan," said Jerome with a chuckle. "He's always encouraged me. When we were only fourteen, he was saying, ' Jerome, you've got to go to university. You're simply wasting your brains if you don't.' And you know? He's right."

"He's a good friend," said Rebecca, thoughtfully. "I'd like a friend like him."

"You mean you don't have such a friend?" Jerome looked surprised.

"I'm not a particularly social person, Jerome. It's not easy for me to meet people. Not like Jeanette. She walks into a room, and lights up the place. I envy her that. Had she not introduced us, I'd be sitting quietly in a corner, nervously caressing a glass of juice. I can see you look surprised."

"I am. You look so poised, so self-possessed. I can't imagine your having difficulty meeting people."

"Obviously, Alan didn't tell you that about me. He's such a gentle person," said Rebecca, with a soft smile. "But he probably told you about my horses."

"As a matter of fact he did. He told me how much you love to ride, and the pleasure you get out of looking after them."

"He's right. The two of us have been for rides together, though he's not exactly comfortable on a horse." Rebecca smiled at Jerome.

"You know something Rebecca? Neither would I," added Jerome, laughing.

"Well then, I'll just have to let you try."

"You mean you're going to have me sit on a horse?" said Jerome, incredulously.

"There's always a first time, Jerome."

"I don't think I've even touched a horse, let alone sit on one."

"So, I'm going to have the distinct pleasure of providing you with a first," said Rebecca, enthusiastically.

"Well now, I'm going to have to think about this," Jerome answered slowly.

"I tell you what. You come for a ride, and after, you can treat me to a performance of Bach on our grand piano. Alan told me how well you play Bach. That might even impress my mother."

"Never did I think I would be bribed to ride a horse," Jerome answered with a chuckle.

Just then Alan appeared looking happy and relaxed. In one hand he held a plate of small sandwiches, their crusts neatly sliced off.

" You two look to be getting along well," he said jovially." Here, try one. Egg salad. Made them myself. Delicious."

"I will," said Rebecca. "And one for Jerome. Alan, you're so domesticated."

"I know. I know. I'd make someone a wonderful wife," Alan replied blandly.

"Alan. Before you disappear, I want you to know, Rebecca has bribed me to ride one of her horses. One ride equals one session on her grand piano. You failed to tell me your cousin is so persuasive."

"Well, I hope you take to horses better than I did. I still find them rather intimidating. When is this event to take place?"

"Next weekend," interjected Rebecca.

Jerome looked surprised. "You see Alan. I have no say in the matter."

Rebecca was laughing softly. Jerome knew she was amused at how easily he had succumbed to her proposal. Already he felt she was beginning to like him.

"Well," said Alan, "you'll love the piano."

The rest of the evening, Jerome talked with friends and acquaintances, but rarely did his eyes leave Rebecca for long.

Before leaving, he thanked Alan and Jeanette for the party, then before saying goodnight to Rebecca, he made arrangements with her about the ride. She would phone him, but he declined her offer to pick him up. He would take the bus. The service was good. The truth was he did not want Mrs.Millden driving up to his simple home in her new Daimler. Jerome had his pride.

For the first time in his life Jerome was sitting astride a horse, hoping he would not make some undignified display of equestrian ineptitude.

"You know, Rebecca, you're privileged to own horses," Jerome said a little bluntly.

"I realize that, and I appreciate having them," answered Rebecca in a soft, firm voice.

"My apology. I didn't mean to sound judgmental." Jerome looked a little sheepish. "Sometimes my social views take over. OK Rebecca. You lead slowly, and I'll follow."

The maples and sycamores raised their leafless branches to a grey, overcast sky. Even here winter was bleak. Though there was peacefulness in these woods above the river, Jerome longed for the fresh greenness of spring. Soon Rebecca moved the horses to a trot, and as they approached a large field, she gave Jerome instructions on what to do as the horses began a canter. He adapted well to the movement of the horse, and found the experience quite invigorating.

"You're a quick learner, Jerome," remarked Rebecca, as they slowed to a trot. "You seem to be enjoying yourself."

"It's the cowboy in me bursting to come out," said Jerome with a broad grin. "I guess I was born too late," he continued, assuming a John Wayne posture in the saddle. Rebecca was laughing, and the look in her soft, blue eyes revealed the warm feeling that possessed her whole body. Never had she experienced this before.

They returned the horses to the stables, rubbed them down, and fed them.

"Such a lot of work," commented Jerome.

"Yes," agreed Rebecca, "but they're worth it. I love them, and they give me such pleasure."

As they walked back to Rebecca's home, Jerome could not help but think how privileged Rebecca was—affluent parents, private school, beautiful home, and horses. Yet she remained unspoiled. There was about her an appealing naivete. He realized he was growing very fond of her. At nearly eighteen he didn't think he would ever feel this way about someone, but he liked the feeling. Then quite spontaneously, Rebecca linked her arm through his.

"Do you realize Rebecca, I'm about to meet your mother for the first time. I need you to prepare me for this occasion. Already I'm feeling nervous."

"I've been thinking about that, though I think you'll pass with flying colours."

"Even though I live in Eldon, and my father is a bus driver?"

"Even though you live in Eldon, and your father is a bus driver," repeated Rebecca emphatically. "Having said that, I must tell you mother is not the most tactful person. She's very class conscious, especially with people below her social standing. Try not to be too annoyed with her." Then Rebecca stopped, and looked at Jerome. "I'd like for us to be good friends," she said, her eyes filling with tears.

"I would like that very much," replied Jerome.

Independently wealthy, and an unmitigated snob, Florence Millden was tall, beautiful, and unabashedly self-centered. Women were jealous of her, men desired her, and the few friends Rebecca had shunned her. Jerome would soon be one of the latter. That Rebecca had remained uninfluenced by her mother never ceased to amaze those who knew both mother and daughter.

"Mother, I'd like you to meet Jerome. He's a friend of Alan. They've known each other for years." Rebecca made her introduction quietly.

"Hello Jerome." Mrs. Millden looked enquiringly at him. "And where do you live "?

"In Eldon, Mrs.Millden."

"Oh, that's where the council houses are, I believe," stated Mrs. Millden condescendingly.

Jerome winched. This was going to be one of those social interrogations.

"Do you live in one of those houses"? Mrs. Millden asked imperiously.

"As a matter of fact I do," answered Jerome, adding somewhat facetiously, "with my parents and my younger sister and brother."

"Oh dear. Rather small for five people, isn't it, Jerome"? Her tone was decidedly patronizing.

Embarrassed by her mother's questioning, Rebecca interrupted. "Excuse me mother. I think Jerome has to catch a bus."

"Your parents don't have a car"? Mrs. Millden's question was purely rhetorical.

"No. It's a luxury they as yet have not been able to afford."

"Most unfortunate. I really don't know what I would do without one. I'd drive you, but it's getting dark, and I'm a little uncertain of the way, especially in the dark."

"Thank you, Mrs. Millden. I enjoy the bus ride. Gives me time to think. Goodbye Mrs. Millden,"

"Goodbye Jerome." Mrs. Millden's smile was blatantly contrived.

Rebecca walked Jerome to the bus stop. "I must apologize for my mother's tactlessness. I get so annoyed with her sometimes. We really clash on this class issue." Rebecca could not conceal her anger.

"Thanks for interrupting. I see what you mean about the class consciousness. I was certain your mother's next question was going to be about my father's occupation."

"That will come. In fact, I'm sure mother will ask me as soon as I return."

"Tell her my father circumnavigates the town in order to facilitate the movement of people. That should make her think a little," said Jerome with a broad grin.

"Now that would totally confuse my mother, though she might conclude I was being quite impertinent." Rebecca gave special emphasis to the last two words.

There was a bus at the stop when they arrived, but before Jerome boarded, Rebecca touched his arm. "Jerome, don't let my mother come between us." There was an appealing softness in her eyes. He returned her gaze, and quietly replied, "No Rebecca. I promise you I will not. Thank you for a beautiful day."

The bus started up, and quickly drove away, leaving Rebecca bathed in the yellow light of a street lamp.

Two days after his initiation to horse riding, Jerome was talking to Alan.

"Jerome, how was the horse riding?"

"The horse riding was great. I really enjoyed it. Mother was a different story. It's clear your aunt does not approve of her daughter associating with the son of a bus driver."

"Who lives in a council house in Eldon," Alan added.

"Exactly. Obviously, Rebecca and her mother have considerable disagreement over social class. Her mother is adamant about Rebecca's associating only with people at her social level. I can see now why your parents are infrequent visitors to your aunt."

"I haven't been to Rebecca's home in months. Jeanette never goes, even though she and Rebecca get on well. My aunt turns people off, which is why she has so few friends."

"I wonder she has any," snapped Jerome. "But I still intend to see Rebecca."

"I'm pleased about that. I think Rebecca needs a friend like you."

"I'll stick around, Alan. That's a promise."

Covered in beech trees and sycamore trees, the gently rolling Choswell Hills slope down to the north bank of the Tarnley River. They were favourite haunts for Jerome and Rebecca, who welcomed their lush spring greenery, and admired their spectacular autumn blaze. Sometimes though, they strolled along the path that follows the long meanders of the river, interrupted in places where it drops suddenly, by locks. The most famous of these was Maudlin, noted for its beautiful gardens and artistic floral displays. Responsible for this was John Trethewey. For twenty years his artistry and dedication had won him prizes, as well as the hearts of thousands of admirers, who annually made their pilgrimage to view John's latest creations. When Jerome and Rebecca first met John, he took an instant liking to them.

"Hello young people. Enjoying the spring sun?" John's voice was cheerful, and richly baritone. He was carefully administering plant food to some nasturtiums. With a grimace, he straightened up. "Ah," he groaned. "Getting too old for this, and too stiff." He smiled at them with twinkling blue eyes. "I'm John Trethewey," he announced, and touched his broad-brimmed hat as he nodded at Rebecca. "I'm the lock-keeper and gardener."

"I'm Jerome, and this is my friend, Rebecca."

"Well now, I'm pleased to meet you."

"We've come to admire your latest creation, John. We know you have a different design each year," said Jerome.

"Indeed I do. That's one of the challenges of this work. It keeps my mind active."

"I think it's great to have such creative work," said Jerome with growing interest. "You must spend hours working in your garden."

"Indeed I do, Jerome. But as they say, 'it's a labour of love,'" and a smile lit up his dark, creased face. "I get great pleasure from doing this, and I know it gives great pleasure to the people who visit here. That's the wonderful thing about my work, sharing it with others. Now, how many people can say that about their work"? John looked at the two of them and smiled.

"Not many," answered Jerome. "All praise, no complaints. Wouldn't my father like that"?

"And what does your father do?"

"He's a bus driver in town," replied Jerome, flatly.

"And he's very good," added Rebecca.

"Well Jerome, your father performs useful work, and I'm afraid people like your father aren't appreciated enough."

"He sits in his cab up front, and never talks to anyone, whereas you, John, get to talk to everyone who comes to visit your gardens to admire the flowers. You talk about your work. My father just drives. No questions asked." There was resentment in Jerome's voice.

"Does your father have a garden?" asked John quietly.

"We live in a council house in Eldon, John," was Jerome's quick response. "Only the pavement in front, and not much in the back,"

"Oh, that's most unfortunate," said John, his voice full of compassion.

"Everyone should have a garden. It's God's photo album." For a moment he seemed in thought. Then, looking at Rebecca, he asked, "Do you have a garden, Rebecca?"

"I do It's rather big."

"Rather," interrupted Jerome, "means just over an acre."

"An acre!" That's a park. Where do you live?"

"In Riverview Heights,"

Then John looked closely at the two of them. Jerome understood that look. Clearly, John was wondering why a girl living in Riverview Heights was going with a boy from Eldon. If such a thought was going through John's mind, he tactfully refrained from asking questions.

"Now don't you leave," said John, and disappearing around the back of his house, he reappeared minutes later, holding a beautiful bouquet of assorted flowers in his large hands. "These are for your parents," he said, handing the bouquet to Jerome. "I was going to say, give them to your mother, but your father might not have appreciated that," he said with a mischievous chuckle. Jerome thanked John, and smiled. He enjoyed John's sense of humour.

"My parents will be delighted with these."

"Now Rebecca, you wont be offended if I don't give you some flowers?

With a garden the size of yours, you could start a nursery."

Rebecca laughed. "My mother would probably give them to her cleaning lady."

"Well, young people, I've enjoyed talking with you. Now I must get back to my garden, but come again soon." He tipped his hat to Rebecca, and said, "Good-day to you both." Then he walked slowly toward a flowerbed some distance away.

In the late spring of 1948, a memorable event in Jerome's social life was an invitation to dinner at the home of Mr. and Mrs. Millden. This event truly defined the economic and social differences between the two families.

The dinner was a mixture of inquisition and pleasant conversation. Rebecca's mother was the inquisitor, and her father provided the pleasant conversation. The dinner table was a display of upper class dining propriety. Jerome was both impressed and uneasy. He realized Mrs. Millden was making a statement about upper class cuisine and dining etiquette. She had even retained the services of her young maid, Lucy, to serve the dinner. Jerome responded appropriately.

Mr. Millden said a short, very traditional grace; then Mrs. Millden looked at Jerome, and said, "I'm sure you like filet mignon. Every so often we indulge a little." Her tone was decidedly supercilious.

"I regret, our budget does not allow such extravagance, Mrs. Millden, so this is something of a luxury for me."

Rebecca cast a disapproving look at her mother, and commented that she had considered becoming a vegetarian.

"Really dear, what prompted that idea?"

"Oh, I've been reading about the benefits of a vegetarian diet."

"Well dear, we'll let Jerome savour the benefits of filet mignon, since he doesn't get the opportunity at home."

Jerome chewed a small piece of his steak while considering Mrs. Millden's comment.

Clearly uncomfortable with the dietary conversation, Mr. Millden looked at Jerome. "Rebecca tells me you're a math whiz, and hope to win a scholarship to Cambridge, Jerome."

"Well sir, 'hope' is the operative word. I believe I have a distinct possibility of winning a scholarship. My results to date indicate that." Jerome thought his response a little wordy, but Mr. Millden pursued the matter.

"Tell me Jerome, what will you do with a degree in mathematics?"

Mrs. Millden appeared suddenly to be very interested.

"There is the possibility of my teaching at a university, or I could pursue a career in actuarial science, probably with a major insurance company."

"Most interesting. Wonderful options. Which one do you favour?"

"From a purely monetary point of view, actuarial science."

"Ah, yes. Unfortunately, money is important in our society," said Mr. Millden, almost apologetically.

"My dear, it's absolutely essential. Without it, one just doesn't experience life." Mrs. Millden chose this opportune moment to enter the conversation. "We're so fortunate that you darling, and your father and grandparents were such clever people." As Mrs. Millden made this last statement she looked at Jerome and smiled.

"Yes, you are indeed, most fortunate," said Jerome, and with a hint of sarcasm, added, "Obviously, my grandparents weren't so clever."

Sensing a growing tension, Mr. Millden quietly intervened. "But you know, Jerome, you'll change all that. I think you'll be successful in life, as will others of your generation from similar circumstances."

"I hope so sir. At least I intend to try."

"Oh, you'll do more than try," answered Mr. Millden with a smile.

"Tell me Jerome, have you ever thought of a career in law? With your mind you'd make an excellent lawyer, and I'd be delighted to have you article in my firm. You should think seriously about it."

"Thank you for the offer, Mr. Millden, but I think I'd make a better mathematician. At least, I believe I'm far more suited to that field of endeavour. But I will think about your suggestion."

"Certainly dear, were Jerome coming from a family like yours with its extensive legal background it would help considerably. But you must remember dear, he doesn't have that advantage." Mrs. Millden smiled condescendingly at Jerome.

"Well, my dear, I really don't think family background has much to do with it, but intellectual ability does, and it seems to me that in that regard, Jerome is eminently qualified." Mrs. Millden's smile quickly vanished.

"But Jerome, Rebecca tells me you intend to immigrate to America after you graduate."

"Yes sir, that's my intention," replied Jerome.

At this point Mrs. Millden interrupted, and asked Lucy to serve dessert. Mr. Millden was quite agreeable, but continued his line of inquiry with a request. "Jerome, call me Mr. Millden, I prefer it to 'sir.'"

"Very well, sir, oh, Mr. Millden," Jerome responded, a broad smile on his face. Mr. Millden laughed approvingly. He was obviously enjoying Rebecca's young friend. Mrs. Millden was less amused.

"Well, to continue, Mr. Millden, I do intend to immigrate to America."

Suddenly, Mrs. Millden interjected. "Why would you want to do that, Jerome? Americans are so uncouth, so brash. And America seems such a superficial country. Why would you not want to remain in England where there is so much more culture?" She smiled condescendingly as she said this. Before Jerome could respond, Rebecca interrupted.

"Mother, I'm sure not all Americans are uncouth and brash. In fact, we don't even know any. And I'm sure there's a lot of culture in America. Just look at all those incredible musicals now playing in London that people are flocking to."

"Well, my dear," her mother replied, a little taken aback by Rebecca's criticism, "one doesn't have to know people in order to know about them."

Jerome was unimpressed with Mrs. Millden's observations of America. He returned her smile, and began, "America is a much more open society than is England. I see it as truly a land of opportunity. It's not bound by such social conventions as exist here in England. What school you attend, and what your father does are of little concern. What is more important is what you can do. What you believe you can achieve." Jerome realized he was launching into a tirade against his country's social system. A frown from Rebecca was a clear sign to back off.

"You doubtless have other views, Mr. Millden," said Jerome. The answer surprised him

"You know, Jerome, our system has been very wasteful of its youth. The changes in the education system are benefiting so many of our young people who formerly would have been denied today's opportunities. Why, you're a perfect example. Bus driver's son wins scholarship to Cambridge. You have ambition, and that's good. You'll go a long way." Mr. Millden smiled warmly at Jerome.

"My dear," said Mrs. Millden, "I didn't realize you held such views."

"That, my dear, is because you choose not to discuss such issues." Mrs. Millden looked decidedly crestfallen, and remained silent. Jerome decided to ease the tension.

"Mrs. Millden, that was a most delicious dinner, and I thank you very much. It was a culinary experience."

"Well, thank you, Jerome. I'm pleased you appreciated it." Mrs. Millden was clearly delighted with the compliment. He shook hands with Mr. Millden, and thanked him for a most interesting evening.

"A pleasure talking with you Jerome. I admire young people who articulate their ideas well; all the best in those exams, Jerome. I'm sure you'll do very well. Now you drop by again."

"Thank you sir, oh, Mr. Millden." They laughed together.

On the way to the bus, Jerome turned to Rebecca, and said, "I really like your father. I felt comfortable in his presence. He wasn't judging me the way your mother does." "My father's always been like that. I can remember near the end of the war, he said, 'Things have got to change when the war's over. This country wastes too many of its youth.' My mother didn't understand what he meant, and chose to ignore him. I think he should have explained, but he didn't." "That's unfortunate. Somehow though, I don't think your mother would have understood." "I have to admit, you're right," A bus was waiting at the stop. Before boarding, Jerome held Rebecca's hands, and thanked her for a beautiful evening. "I so enjoyed myself," he said. Then, quite suddenly he leaned toward Rebecca, and kissed her lightly on the forehead. She did not kiss him then. Instead, she squeezed his hands, and smiled up at him. "Good night, Jerome."

"Good night, Rebecca. Thanks again. I really did enjoy the evening, especially the filet mignon." Rebecca laughed.

"Mother will be most impressed. Pheasant next time," she added, still laughing.

On the bus, he sat so that he could see Rebecca. She waved as the bus drove away. Jerome returned the wave. Then the bus turned, and she was out of sight, and Jerome was left with his thoughts.

One afternoon early in summer, Jerome and Rebecca returned from a ride through the woods on the Choswell Hills. Rebecca's mother was standing by the Steck grand piano in the spacious drawing room. The keyboard lid was up, and the large top was raised. Mrs. Millden was unusually affable as she greeted Jerome, entering the room with Rebecca.

"Good afternoon, Jerome. Did you enjoy your ride?"

"Yes, I did, Mrs. Millden," replied Jerome, frowning. "It was most relaxing."

"They are beautiful horses, aren't they?" said Mrs. Millden, and without allowing Jerome a reply, she added, "They cost a lot of money."

"I'm sure they did. Rebecca is most fortunate. But then she knows that," said Jerome.

"I hope so," replied Mrs. Millden, a trifle facetiously. "Now Jerome, we have yet to hear you play the piano. I would like to know that you do play," she added rather tactlessly.

"Oh yes, mother, Jerome plays," said Rebecca emphatically. She was visibly annoyed at her mother's remark.

"I'd be pleased to oblige. After all, I don't think your beautiful piano is used very often." Jerome's response was more a rebuttal than an acceptance. "But before I touch those keys, let me first wash my hands."

"Why certainly. Rebecca dear, show Jerome to the bathroom off the hallway."

During their absence, Mrs. Millden busied herself looking through scores for different piano arrangements of works by Beethoven, Bach, Mozart, and Chopin. None of them meant anything to her. They all looked so complicated, and she wondered if Jerome could possibly follow any of them. Rebecca could play some of them, but they were not easy for her.

Jerome and Rebecca entered the room talking quietly to each other. Mrs. Millden approached Jerome, and handed him a number of piano scores.

"Perhaps there is something here that you can play. Although I must say, they all look frightfully complicated. Perhaps we can find you something a little easier." Mrs. Millden's tone was slightly condescending.

"That wont be necessary. I have the music here," and Jerome pointed to his head.

Somewhat perplexed by his response, Mrs.Millden sat down, and watched Jerome intently as he strode toward the piano. He sat down on the padded bench, adjusted its height, and looked intently at the keyboard. His feet touched the pedals lightly, and he placed his long, slender fingers above the keys. Mrs. Millden sat as one entranced. He is really going to play, she thought. Then suddenly, Jerome's fingers were moving deftly over the keyboard in a magnificent rendition of Chopin's Fantasy in C sharp. Mrs. Millden was transfixed. Never had she heard such beautiful playing on this piano. She could not take her eyes off those long fingers that moved with such assurance over the keys. At one moment Jerome's head sank toward the keyboard, then he held it high, eyes closed as he listened intently to the music, which totally absorbed him. When he finished, he placed his hands in his lap, and lowered his head as though contemplating his performance. Visibly surprised and impressed, Mrs. Millden seemed at first to be speechless. Then she said slowly, "Well Jerome, I must say, you play rather well."

"Rather well!" Rebecca was on her feet. "Don't you mean brilliantly? Surely you recognize that, mother?" The tone of her voice emphasized her annoyance. "Last year Jerome earned the highest marks in becoming the youngest Fellow of the Royal Schools of Music, and they don't give that award away, mother." Rebecca could not contain her growing anger.

Mrs. Millden was shaken momentarily by Rebecca's outburst. It was not easy for her to concede that such talent could be found in Eldon. Then Jerome rose, and looking at Mrs. Millden, he said, "Can anything good come out of Eldon?" The biblical allusion was lost on Mrs. Millden, who answered rather hesitantly, "Well, yes, I, er, I suppose so."

"Good day Mrs. Millden," said Jerome as he walked quickly from the room, closely followed by Rebecca. As they reached the front door, she placed her hand on Jerome's arm.

"Please don't let my mother upset you, Jerome," she pleaded. "She's never going to acknowledge your talent, but what is important, I do."

"I know Rebecca. I know," and with that, Jerome left the house, and walked quickly down the driveway to the road. Rebecca watched until he was out of sight. Then she closed the door quietly, and returned to the drawing room. Her mother had not moved.

"You really love him, don't you?" Rebecca's mother spoke in a flat monotone.

"Yes mother, I do." "What is it you don't like about Jerome?"

"Oh darling, it's not that I don't like Jerome. It's just that you're so young to be getting serious about someone. And I do think you should find someone from your own social class, dear. It's so important." She looked at Rebecca.

"Mother, Jerome isn't always going to be in Eldon. Once he's finished university he'll have so many opportunities." Rebecca was becoming irritable, and it was evident in the tone of her voice.

"Now Rebecca dear, please don't get so upset. I'm simply being very honest with you. I've seen what can happen when people from different social classes marry. Divorce can be a nasty thing."

"Divorce! We're not even married, and you're talking divorce. Aren't you jumping to conclusions?" She was becoming increasingly annoyed with her mother.

"I realize that dear," replied her mother, sternly. "I'm merely pointing out what can happen to such marriages. I simply want to make you aware."

"I think Jerome will be too educated for a divorce to happen." By now Rebecca knew she was desperate for any kind of rebuttal.

"Rebecca dear, education has little to do with it. Attitudes die hard, and this is very true of people from Jerome's social class. I would worry about your children. They would have to adjust to two different sets of grandparents. As the children grew older, they would notice the differences and wonder why. They would probably want to see more of your father and me, simply because we could do so much more for them. Don't you see? It would be unfair to the children, and to Jerome's parents." Rebecca's mother was remarkably matter-of-fact.

"I like to think that my children would love both sets of grandparents, even if one lived in Eldon. I think love overlooks class differences."

"Well dear, you do have time to think about what I have said, and I think you will see the truth of what I have told you." There was conviction in her voice.

Rebecca rose slowly, and looking at her mother, said, "I'm going to feed the horses. They need a little more feed after this afternoon's outing."

"Very well dear, while you do that I'll have Lucy prepare some dinner."

"I envy John his contentment. He takes such pride in his gardens, and look at the pleasure his dedication gives others," said Jerome. He and Rebecca were returning from a visit with John Trethewey on a warm, late afternoon in July.

"But you want so much more than that, don't you, Jerome? Beautiful as it is, the garden alone would never satisfy you,"

"You're right, I want so much more than a beautiful flower garden. First, I really want to make something of myself. I want to show people that a bus driver's son can go places, be somebody." His voice was full of passion.

"Oh Jerome, you will. I'm beginning to see why university is so important to you."

"Rebecca, it means everything to me. It's my way out of mediocrity and boredom," said Jerome, passionately. "It's the key to my future; that and immigrating to America."

"You're really serious about going to America, aren't you?" said Rebecca, a tone of regret in her voice.

"But don't you see? I'm going to be the first Callaghan to break free of our social restrictions. I'm going to be the first to make something of himself, to experience real success, to taste affluence." Jerome gesticulated passionately, and Rebecca was amazed at his emotional response. "I watched my grandfather die of TB, after working twenty-five years in the coal- mines. Stay above ground, son,' he told my father, so he became a bus driver." There was sadness in Jerome's dark eyes, and suddenly

Rebecca felt a strong empathy for him. Then, quite unexpectedly, Jerome asked, "Rebecca, do you think you would like living in America?"

Rebecca stopped, a little taken aback by Jerome's question. "I don't know. I've never thought about it." Then, looking at Jerome, she asked, "Is that an indirect invitation to go with you?"

"Well, I suppose it is, in a way," relied Jerome, sheepishly.

"Jerome," said Rebecca inquiringly, "That sounds like a proposal, and I'm not yet sixteen." She stopped, and smiled at him.

"Just think," said Jerome, "you have the honour of being the first female I've ever proposed to," and throwing his arms out wide, he bowed.

Rebecca looked at him, tall, dark, and handsome, a smile lighting up his face, and replied, "Oh, I suppose I'm meant to be flattered. And how do I know I'm the first?" She feigned seriousness.

"My dear," answered Jerome, equally serious, "you'll have to accept my word as a gentleman of honour."

Rebecca was looking at him with softness in her eyes. "Oh darling, I do love you." Tears filled her eyes as she took hold of Jerome's hands.

"Now isn't that a coincidence?" said Jerome. "I feel the same way about you, Rebecca," and he held her close, and touched her hair with his lips. Rebecca looked up, and for the first time they kissed. This was a beautiful moment in their young lives, a wonderful mingling of innocence and love. This was the first admission of their love for each other. Hand in hand, they continued their walk along the river path. For much of the way Rebecca rested her head on Jerome's shoulder. They walked a while in silence before Jerome said, "Rebecca, don't mention any of this to your mother. I don't think she would approve. Bus driver's son proposes to wealthy lawyer's daughter."

Rebecca was laughing as she replied, "Wealthy lawyer's daughter accepts."

Jerome was stunned. For a moment he was speechless. Was this a premature acceptance of marriage? Had the joke played out? Behind the laughter, was Rebecca serious? Then she seemed to read his thoughts.

"Jerome, I can tell what you're thinking. The answer is, ' I'll put it on hold until I finish school.'" Then linking arms with Jerome, she began talking about her horses, and their going for a ride soon. Jerome was uncharacteristically quiet. He had never been in love before, and Rebecca was very special. He never thought that at eighteen he would be so hopelessly in love.

That evening, Jerome had a long talk with his mother about falling in love. At forty, Kathleen Callaghan was still a very attractive woman. Her long black hair fell evenly about her shoulders, and her habit of taking long walks accounted for her glowing complexion. She loved deeply, and laughed a lot, because she believed both were beneficial to good health, and both showed in the warmth of her dark blue eyes. Her full, sensual lips emphasized a beauty that turned many a head. But she was devoted to both her husband and her children. Though she did not play favourites, she was particularly close to Jerome. He was the eldest, and seemed destined to achieve so much. He would be the first Callaghan to go to university, and that would allow him to fulfill the ambitions he talked about, and that drove him to study so hard. Jerome would be much more than a bus driver.

Jerome's mother was busy crocheting when he entered the front room. He slumped down in an easy chair, and stretched out his long legs. "Good evening, Mum. What are you doing?"

Without looking up, she answered quietly, "I'm crocheting for the church bazaar. Now, did you have an enjoyable afternoon with Rebecca?" As she asked the question, she put aside her crocheting. She seemed to anticipate more than a short answer to her question. Jerome was here to talk.

"We visited John at the lock. His gardens are beautiful. He has grown the most gorgeous dahlias and chrysanthemums. You and dad should go and see them."

"We will dear. We could go on Monday. Your father has a day off. I think he'd appreciate visiting the gardens and talking to John. He's such a nice man." She knew Jerome wanted to talk about more than John's gardens. "How is Rebecca?" she asked. Jerome could see his mother wanted more than a one-word answer.

"Rebecca's fine, Mum, replied Jerome. "In fact, she's quite wonderful," he added. His mother was looking intently at him. "Mum, how old were you when you fell in love with Dad?" The question did not surprise his mother.

"I was not much older than you, dear. I was just nineteen, and it was love at first sight. As soon as I saw your father, I knew he was the man for me."

"And you never dated anyone else?" Jerome seemed surprised.

"No, I didn't," Jerome's mother answered with a smile.

"Mum, I thought you would've had a line of young men waiting to date you."

"Oh, there were others, but your father was the one, and I've never regretted my choice." Then looking intently at Jerome, she asked, "Now tell me dear, are you in love with Rebecca?"

"Yes mum, I am. I'm sure I am."

"Oh, my dear. You know when you are. It's a giddy, unreal feeling, and looking at you, I'd say that's what you're experiencing."

"Mum," said Jerome dreamily," you're absolutely right. I should know I can't hide this feeling from you."

"Well, my dear, it doesn't last. It can't. You have to come back to reality."

"Then you marry, and reality takes over," said Jerome, with a smile.

"Exactly dear. You're so righ, but you know, Jerome, that's when the real love begins."

"And that will happen to Rebecca and me?" said Jerome wistfully.

"I like to think so dear," replied his mother. Then her tone changed. "But Jerome, Rebecca's so young. Didn't you tell me she's not yet sixteen?"

"She'll be sixteen next month."

"That's too young to be in love, and too young to be thinking of marriage, Jerome."

"Mum, Rebecca's not thinking marriage. First she's going to finish school, and then she may work for her father." Jerome leaned forward to emphasize his point.

"And you my dear have three years of university once you finish your military service."

"Exactly, mother, and by then I will be twenty-three, and Rebecca will be almost twenty-one, not nineteen," said Jerome, smiling at his mother.

"But I wasn't marrying a university graduate. Your father was just starting to drive buses, and I was secretary to one of the transit supervisors," said his mother quietly.

"You've been wonderful parents." As Jerome said this, he rose, went over to his mother, and hugged her. "Thanks Mum for everything."

She looked into his smiling face, and with tear-filled eyes said,

"You're very welcome my dear. Your father and I are so proud of you."

Jerome walked over to the beautifully preserved upright piano, a cherished family possession, sat down, and began playing Bach's Jesu, Joy of Man's Desiring. It was his mother's favourite. She rested her head on the high back, and she recalled a small boy first playing this piece, stumbling, but never giving up. Now the young man was performing with such virtuosity tears came to her eyes. No, she wasn't worried about Jerome. He was going to be successful in life.

~

Early in August, the inevitable call-up notice arrived. Jerome had decided to forgo the academic exemption granted university entrants, and complete his two years of National Service. He informed Rebecca of his decision.

"Oh Jerome, I think that's a smart decision. Hopefully, you'll be posted somewhere near, and be home most weekends."

"Well, darling, don't count on that," replied Jerome, with a smile. They might decide to send me to some isolated radar post in the Shetland Isles."

"Don't even think of it," said Rebecca, emphatically.

"Just think," added Jerome, "I might meet one of those bonny highland lassies, complete with kilt, flaxen hair, and blue eyes."

"And just where have you been hearing about such lassies?" asked Rebecca, her hands firmly on her hips.

Very softly, Jerome began to sing, "I love a lassie, a bonny, Hieland lassie."

To his surprise, Rebecca responded with, "Speed bonny boat like a bird on the wing, over the sea to Skye," in a soft soprano.

"Rebecca," exclaimed a surprised Jerome, "you never told me you sing, and so well."

"Only in the shower. Now, about that bonny lassie?"

"No problem. I'll have a Shetland pony as a pet, and learn to knit jumpers from Shetland wool," Jerome answered jovially.

"This conversation is becoming ridiculous," said Rebecca, laughing. I wish to remind you that when you finish your National Service, you'll be twenty, and I'll be eighteen, and I'll have to consider that proposal you made to me." Rebecca was smiling, but Jerome was suddenly looking a little stunned.

"But Rebecca," Jerome stammered, "you will be just eighteen. Isn't that rather young to be considering marriage?"

"Exactly, my dear, and you'll have three years of university ahead of you, and by the time you graduate, you'll be a young man of twenty-three, about to launch out into the world." Rebecca was being deliberately histrionic.

"And you, my dear, will no longer be a teenager, and I might just repeat that proposal," Jerome responded.

"Promise!"

Jerome was holding her hands, and looking at her with such love in his eyes. "Promise," he said, softly.

"Oh, Jerome, I do love you." Her voice was a whisper as she held him close for a moment. Then they continued their walk in the warmth of a summer afternoon. The following week, he had to report for National Service. Were it possible to avoid this duty, he would gladly have done so. He understood his father's resentment, "Why should young people have to put their careers on hold to waste two years in the military," he protested.

⌐⌐⌐

Jerome had few opportunities to be home between his conscription into the Air Force for National Service, and his departure to Singapore early in November. Brief as his visits were, they were times of intense happiness for him and Rebecca. The love between them grew. Occasionally, they went for long, leisurely rides, but mostly they walked arm in arm, enjoying the closeness. At times such as these, Jerome dreaded having to return to camp, and Rebecca experienced an emptiness following his departure.

"I hate these partings, Jerome," said Rebecca, early one Sunday afternoon. They had returned from a walk in the fading warmth of a late summer day. The leaves on the Choswell hillsides were showing the first signs of autumn's splendour. "I just hate your leaving. I'm never sure when I'll see you again."

"Rebecca, darling, I feel the same way. More and more, I loathe this conscription. It's a real imposition. I should be studying mathematics at university instead of marching around a parade ground listening to some drill instructor barking out orders." There was deep resentment in Jerome's voice.

"How much longer do you have left of this marching?"

"Two weeks, and then I'll spend a month learning about special electronic equipment. At least it'll be a pleasant change, and I'll have intelligent instructors," Jerome continued, testily.

"I've never heard you so angry. Am I seeing another side of Jerome Callaghan?" asked a surprised Rebecca.

"Not really. It's just that I'm so annoyed at having to waste two years of my life in what is a truly useless programme."

"I understand, darling. I feel for your having to put your plans on hold." Rebecca's voice was soft, and full of compassion. She pulled Jerome close. "And what happens when you've finished your course?"

Jerome's mood changed as he looked at Rebecca, and replied," Don't you remember?" I'm going to some remote posting in Scotland."

"Don't you dare," retorted Rebecca. "I just wont allow it."

"Oh, you and who else?"

"Oh, I'm sure mother knows someone with influence."

"Rebecca, do you really think your mother would intercede on my behalf ? I think she'd be glad to see me so far way." Jerome's face was expressionless.

"Darling, don't be so hard on my mother. I think she would help you if she could. I don't think she dislikes you." There was an uncertainty in Rebecca's voice.

"Now that I find hard to believe."

"Let's not argue, darling," pleaded Rebecca, quietly. "Remember, I once told you not to let my mother come between us."

"I do remember. I promise I wont let that happen," said Jerome, softly. "Your mother may yet surprise me."

"You just never know," said Rebecca, smiling.

"But Rebecca, darling, I have to leave, or I'll miss the bus back to camp."

"Oh, darling, I'll miss you," said Rebecca, tearfully.

They embraced and kissed, and then Jerome left quickly. Prolonged farewells were too emotionally draining.

That autumn was warm and mellow, and summer seemed reluctant to surrender its warmth and greenery to the lavish motley of autumn. Every weekend when Jerome was home, he took time to be with Rebecca. Sometimes they rode the horses, other times they went for leisurely walks along the Chosewell Hills.

"I love this kind of autumn," said Jerome. "' Season of mist and mellow fruitfulness.' Keats described it so well."

"'Close bosom friend of the maturing sun,'" Rebecca added. "We've been studying Keats. Such a short life."

"But he left behind such immortal and memorable poetry," said Jerome.

"Is that what you want to do, Jerome?"

"What, write poetry?"

"No. Leave something memorable behind?"

"I'd love to. Something that is uniquely me, but I don't think it will be poetry."

"What about music?" Rebecca was intent on pursuing the subject.

"No. I play, but I don't compose. I tried composing short piano pieces, but I'm no Mozart or Beethoven. They were geniuses."

"And there's only been one Mozart, and one Beethoven," Rebecca continued.

"And that's all there'll ever be. They are truly unique," added Jerome, emphatically. "I guess I'll have to settle for much less."

Rebecca looked at him with love in her eyes. "Just be a good man."

"Thank you, Rebecca, I'll try."

When they reached the house, they entered, and Jerome went over to the piano, sat down, and began to play a Beethoven sonata. Very soon, Rebecca's mother entered quietly, sat down, and listened to the music. Rebecca was seated on the floor, and reclining against a large easy chair. Her eyes were closed. Her mother was totally absorbed in Jerome's playing. It was beautiful. As if by magic she was in another world. The music was hypnotic. It was in such a state that she wrestled with what to her was a seeming paradox. Could such talent come out of Eldon? Could it really come from the offspring of a bus driver? For her the compromise was difficult. Yet Jerome stirred something within her. He played so beautifully, and with such emotion. She found herself envying him his gift. If only his father were a doctor, or a corporate lawyer, or a successful businessman. A bus driver just wasn't good enough. It was as inconceivable to her to consider visiting the Callaghans, as it was for her to consider inviting them to her home. She believed that were the Callaghans to visit her and her husband, the experience would be very unsettling for the Callaghans. They simply would be most uncomfortable with the class difference. Indeed, it was her belief that Jerome's mother would be decidedly uncomfortable. In this respect, she greatly misjudged Kathleen Callaghan.

All this speculation by Mrs. Millden was of no real consequence, because the Callaghans and the Milldens never did meet, socially or otherwise.

A few days before Jerome completed the electronics course, he was informed of his posting to Singapore. It came as a surprise. Apparently, there was a need for technicians with his particular skills. He would travel to a base in northwest England, and sail from the port of Liverpool. Jerome had mixed feelings about the posting. Singapore sounded exciting, almost exotic. It would provide a very dramatic change in his life; certainly better than some dreary camp in England. But he would miss Rebecca. They loved each other very much. This kind of separation would be hard on both of them, though it would test the sincerity of their emotions. Jerome knew his parents would be especially sad at his going so far away. Strong as his mother was, she would worry about her son, and would pray for him daily. Another person Jerome would miss was John Trethewey. John and he had become close friends. John always welcomed Jerome warmly, and took obvious pride in showing Jerome his latest floral arrangements, and informing him about next spring's garden designs. Mostly though, John appreciated Jerome's genuine interest in his horticultural work.

Before leaving for Singapore, Jerome paid John a final visit. He was busy preparing seedlings for next spring's gardens. As usual, they were going to be a rainbow of colours.

"So Jerome, you're going to Singapore. Now that's a long way from here. You take care of yourself." John was emotional, and tears misted his eyes. "I've come to think of you as the son I never had." There was a tremor in his voice. "Send me a card now and then. I'd really like that, Jerome."

"I'll do that, John. I want to know how your gardens are doing, and how many thousands of visitors you have. So keep count, John." Jerome smiled. Then he took John's hand warmly, and put his arm around John's shoulder. "Goodbye John. It's been a pleasure visiting you and enjoying the beauty of your gardens."

"Thank you. I appreciate the interest you have shown in my work. Now remember, send me a card occasionally."

"I promise," said Jerome, and with that he left, and began to walk back along the river path. He turned before the path meandered out of sight of the lock. John was still watching him. Jerome waved, and John returned the wave enthusiastically. Then Jerome turned and disappeared from John's sight. Jerome would never see him again.

The time came for Jerome to say goodbye to Rebecca. The parting was predictably sad. Mrs.Millden's farewell was polite and formal. "Take care of yourself, Jerome, and do write to us occasionally, won't you?" She smiled at him, but did not shake his hand.

"Oh, I will write, frequently, Mrs.Millden. You can be assured of that."

"I suppose Rebecca will keep us informed," said Mrs. Millden, with a smile. Then she turned and walked inside. Somehow, Jerome felt this really was goodbye. Unfortunately, Rebecca's father was away at a law conference in Bournemouth. He would most certainly have given Jerome a warm farewell. He told Rebecca to do so for him. Just then, Rebecca took Jerome's arm, and together they began to walk to the bus. A short distance down the road, Rebecca turned unexpectedly into a narrow, hedge-lined lane. Then she put her arms around Jerome, and held him tightly. He returned her embrace. She looked at Jerome with tear-filled eyes,

"Oh, Jerome, darling, I love you so much. I will miss you terribly. You're going so far away, and it seems for so long."

Then she kissed him, and for the first time in a long while, Jerome cried. Never had he felt this way about anyone.

"Rebecca, darling, I feel the same way about you. You've brought me so much happiness. But I'll write every week. Before you know it, I'll be back."

Then they resumed their walk to the bus. The light of a damp November day was fading, and the street- lights were already on. When Jerome and Rebecca reached the stop, a bus was waiting, its engine idling. They held each other, reluctant to let go.

"Come on, now," said the conductor in a loud voice. You'll see her tomorrow."

They kissed a last time, and Jerome boarded the bus. He looked at the conductor,

"I'm afraid I wont see her tomorrow. In three days I leave for Singapore."

"Singapore! Blimey mate! My brother was there during the war. It's a long way from here. You stand right here and wave goodbye to your lady friend."

He left Jerome to be alone on the platform. Jerome waved to Rebecca, and blew her a kiss, which she returned enthusiastically, with tears in her eyes. Then the bus began to slowly drive away. Jerome remained on the platform waving, until the bus turned a corner, and Rebecca disappeared from sight.

Jerome went to Eldon train station alone. Better, he thought, to say goodbye to his family at home. He did not want to prolong such a sad departure. For Jessica, his fifteen-year-old sister, this farewell was a tearful event. She was mature for her age, and sensitive, and she was particularly fond of her elder brother.

"Stay with the studies, sis. You know you're capable of winning a scholarship, don't you?"

"I will, Jerome. I promise," answered Jessica. "But I'll miss you," and she threw her arms around him, and hugged him tightly.

"Wow! He's not your boy friend," said younger brother, Peter. He was much more intrigued with Jerome's going on such a long sea voyage, which would take him through the Suez Canal.

"Jerome, send me a post card from Suez, wont you?"

"Your brother's going ten thousand miles away, and all you can say is 'send me a card from Suez.' What kind of a brother are you? Now give your brother a big hug, and tell him you'll miss him." Mr. Callaghan spoke with a firm voice.

Peter blushed, looked sheepishly at his brother, and hugged him awkwardly.

"I love you little brother." Then turning to his father, he hugged him warmly' "I love you, Dad."

"And I love you, son. You know your mother and I are very proud of you. Stay out of trouble, and don't do anything we wouldn't approve of. Come back safely to us. Remember, you'll be going to Cambridge soon after you return. Then you can really get on with your life." Tears were running down his cheeks.

Finally, Jerome went to his mother. She was sobbing quietly. "I shouldn't cry. It's not going to help you any, Jerome. But, oh, we'll miss you. I'll have no one to play to me of an evening. Try to practice, won't you, dear," she said, with a weak smile.

"I most certainly will, mum."

"And dear," his mother continued, "pray. Pray each day, and ask the Lord to protect you." She put her arms around Jerome, and held him close. "And remember, write often. We'll want to hear all about Singapore, and what you're doing." She pulled his head down, and kissed him. Jerome tasted her salty tears.

"I will mum, I promise. I'll pray every day, and write every week."

Heaving his kit bag onto his shoulder, Jerome walked toward the front door.

"I'll open the door, Jerome," shouted Peter.

Jerome stepped out into the street, turned, and cried out, "Goodbye, wonderful family." Then he was on his way, striding quickly to the bus stop, the cries of his family growing ever fainter.

The night before embarking on the troopship for Singapore, Jerome phoned Rebecca. The phone rang twice before an all too familiar voice answered, "Hello."

"Hello, Rebecca."

"Jerome! "answered an excited Rebecca. "How wonderful to hear your voice. I just knew you'd call. When do you leave?"

"Tomorrow. The ship is due to sail at 13.00 hours. That's one o'clock to you. Three weeks on a ship with hundreds of other young servicemen. It'll have its moments, I suppose, but I'll be glad when it's over."

"Oh, darling, you'll find things to do, and think of all those new places you'll see. I envy you, but I'll also miss you."

"It's going to be a great new experience, but it's a long time to be away from each other," replied Jerome. "This is the last opportunity we'll have to talk to each other for a long time." Jerome's voice was becoming thick with emotion. "Being with you has been wonderful."

"Jerome, I've loved every moment with you. I'm going to miss you so much. Remember, write often, and tell me about everything. You'll have so much to say. I'm going to keep your letters in a special file, and I'll be able to reread them."

"I'll have to be especially careful what I write."

"And Jerome, remember, I'm your girlfriend. No flirting with the local girls." There was humour in Rebecca's voice.

"No friendly associations?"

"Not too friendly," chuckled Rebecca. "Seriously darling, you're going far away, and there'll be all sorts of, well you know, distractions, oh, temptations." Her voice grew suddenly tearful.

"I'll keep you in my thoughts daily. Rebecca dear, I have to say goodbye." His voice was soft and emotional. "I know dear." Rebecca could not hold back her tears. "I told myself I wouldn't cry. I love you, Jerome. Goodbye, and take care of yourself."

"Goodbye Rebecca. Love you," He heard a buzz at the other end, and he hung up the receiver. Many years would pass before they spoke to each other again.

End. Part I.

Part II.

SINGAPORE: JEROME AND FRANCINE

THE VOYAGE provided Jerome some pleasant, unexpected surprises. Many of the conscripts shared his concerns. He met others, who, like himself, had deferred university entry in order to complete their National Service. The passage through the Suez Canal was a revelation. Egyptian vendors in a flotilla of flat-bottomed boats assailed the conscripts with a variety of colourful epithets, to buy their numerous bargains. The closing act between these two opposing groups was indelibly etched in Jerome's mind. With unerring aim, a brash young recruit hurled a heavy china mug at an unsuspecting vendor. The mug shattered to pieces against the man's head. He let forth a stream of unintelligible invectives at his assailant. The ship steamed on, as raucous laughter greeted the enraged victim. It was a manifest act of contempt, by one, ignorant of the Englishman's decades of imposed superiority on an alien people.

Aden, hot and dry, offered a welcome break from shipboard life. Here, Jerome mailed his first letter to Rebecca. The Indian Ocean was rough, but Jerome learned the best way of combating seasickness was to go up on deck and watch the ocean in its turbulent wrath. At Columbo, he was able to mail a second letter to Rebecca. He was keeping his promise of a letter a week. Finally, after three weeks, the ship docked in the hot humidity of Singapore. For the young conscripts, out of England for the first time, this tropical climate was a shock. For Jerome, it was one of many blessings.

Along with other Air Force conscripts, Jerome was bussed to the Changi Air Force base on the southeast side of the island. The barrack block Jerome was assigned to accommodated the members of 205 Transport Squadron, a congenial group of young men, some conscripts, some regulars who had signed on for periods ranging mostly between five and eight years. This was to be home for the next eighteen months, and already Jerome was beginning to feel comfortable. Now, knowing his mailing address, he sent his third letter to Rebecca. She should be pleased with my output, he thought.

From an early age Jerome had learned the mysteries of radio, and had built his first one by age ten. His father, believing there was a great future in this growing technology, encouraged Jerome to persist with his interest. "I'll help you as much as I can with the money," he told Jerome, and his interest never waned. On the squadron, Jerome's job was to service all the air radar equipment, and attend to any necessary repairs. He quickly gained a reputation for his ability to diagnose problems and fix them, which brought with it a variety of nicknames: Whiz Kid, Mr. Fix It, Radar Jerry, and The Fix-it Kid. Each was an indictor of his popularity on the squadron, and the respect he quickly earned.

Rather quickly, Jerome developed a strong fascination for the city of Singapore. He loved the broad boulevards, the lush parklands with their exotic tropical plants, and the fragrance of frangipani that filled the warm tropical nights. So many of the young conscripts around him counted the days to their return to England. They were homesick for their small towns, the pubs, fish and chips, and football matches on Saturdays. Jerome missed none of this. Military life on the island had a freedom absent from that in England. Here, in the ramshackle village of Changi, Jerome could board a bus for the city, and not return until the early hours of Monday morning.

One Saturday, early in March, Jerome arrived back at the barrack block around 10.30. p.m. He had spent a long day in the city visiting a number of attractions including Saint Andrews Cathedral, Parliament House, and Queen Victoria Theatre, on the other side of Saint Andrew's Road. Before taking the bus back to Changi, Jerome decided to wander through the infamous Bugis Street area of Singapore. He had heard much about its notorious reputation from Josh Quinn, a Squadron member. Following his visit to the Singapore Art Museum, Jerome had eaten at an inexpensive Indian restaurant on Bras Basah Road. Bugis Street was only a few blocks away. The walk would be good for digestion, Jerome reasoned. The scent of frangipani filled the night air. Red and yellow hibiscus was visible beneath the yellow street- light. Then he was past the Goddess of Mercy Chinese Temple, and a young, brightly dressed Malay woman emerged from the shadow of a doorway. Jerome looked at her heavily painted face that masked her youthful beauty and her lost innocence. She smelled of cheap perfume.

"You want a good time mister?"

Surprised by this sudden solicitation, Jerome stammered a refusal.

"You don't want me mister? I'm not pretty?" There was a pleading in her questions. "I give you a good time. Good price," she pleaded with a smile.

Jerome shook his head, smiled softly. "No thank you," and he continued on down the flesh market of Bugis Street. He felt besieged. Young Chinese and Malay women propositioned him, eager to sell sex at a negotiated price. Some cursed him for refusing; others were indifferent, knowing a willing customer would soon come.

Bugis Street was a paradox. For most it was a street of short-lived pleasure, but for some, its associated diseases would mean a slow, lingering death. Jerome paused briefly, and looked back. Already, ones he had refused were snuggling up to smiling clients. He walked on out of Bugis Street. A wave of depression overcame him. He never went back.

At the far end of the floor of Barrack Block 124 a group of the boys was clustered around one of the beds. A single light was on, and there was the murmur of conversation. Josh Quinn's voice was distinctly audible. Jerome was quietly approaching his bed, when Josh invited him to join the group. "We're the only ones in tonight," said Josh.

"Unusual for you to be in on a Saturday night, isn't it, Josh?"

"I'm broke," replied Josh, with a grin.

"I could've loaned you money."

"Thank you Jerome, but no thank you. I just have to learn to do without certain pleasures sometimes."

Jerome smiled. He knew what Josh was alluding to.

"Where've you been?" asked Josh.

"I've been wandering around Singapore. Visited the Singapore Art Museum, and ate at an inexpensive Indian restaurant near Bras Basar Road. Then I caught the bus for the thriving metropolis of Changi."

"No detours for ladies of the night?" asked Josh with a smile.

"No Josh. I don't have your audacity. I fear the possible consequences."

Josh smiled sheepishly. "You know, Jerome, you're smart. Do you have a girl friend back home?""

"When I left I did. But now I don't think I do."

"Sent you a 'dear John letter,' eh?" said Josh.

"No Josh, that's just it. She hasn't replied to any of my letters. Since arriving in Singapore, I've written her eight times.

"She's found someone else, Jerome."

"No, I don't think that's what's happened. I think the problem is an interfering and controlling mother. You see my girl friend, Rebecca, comes from a very affluent family. Her father's a corporate lawyer with a successful practice, and her mother is independently wealthy. I live in a council house, and my dad's a bus driver. Josh, I come from the wrong side of the tracks, and the mother let me know it."

"But Jerome, obviously Rebecca didn't mind that you come from the wrong side of the tracks." Josh was clearly interested in Jerome's plight.

"Oh, no. In fact, she strongly disagreed with her mother about class differences. Rebecca looked at the person, not the social class."

"So you think the mother has intercepted and destroyed your letters?"

"It wouldn't surprise me. She's capable of doing that."

"What a bitch!" said Geordie Mathers, angrily. He held strong social views, and had been listening intently. "Can you not write to someone, and find out?"

"I don't want to involve others."

"Well now, Jerome, do you nae have a photie of the lass?" Jock Lockerbie spoke with a thick Glaswegian accent, which drew wry comments from the guys

"I do," replied Jerome. "It's in my locker."

"Well now Jerome, dinae be shy. Let's have a look at the lass."

"Do I have to Jock?"

"Why of course, Jerome. We're family here, are we not lads?" said a smiling Jock. Agreement was unanimous.

Jerome went over to his locker, and returned with a large photograph of Rebecca. She was seated on one of her horses, smiling and relaxed.

"Wow! She's beautiful," said Josh. "But you didn't tell us about the horses."

"Oh, she's a bonny lass indeed," said Jock. "I'd nae be wanting to let go of her." Jock had a broad smile on his face.

Jerome blushed. "It looks as though I'll have to."

"Well Jerome, I'll tell you what to do," said Jock. "You find yourself a lovely wee local lass, and bury your sorrows. These local lassies can be wonderfully sympathetic you know. You'll feel better in no time."

"You really think that would work, Jock?"

"Guaranteed," replied Jock, an oafish smile on his face.

"Maybe I'll meet someone in my travels around the island."

"You just might. The way you're exploring this island, that could easily happen." Josh was serious in his support of Jerome. He knew local women were not an answer to Jerome's loss. "Just sit down, and play the piano the way you did for us the other night." An enigmatic smile lit up Josh's face.

"First, I have to find a piano in an appropriate setting."

"Raffles Hotel," responded Josh.

"Not my class, Josh."

"Oh, right," said Josh, and with an impish smile, added, "you could always try Bugis Street."

"Josh, I'm not that desperate."

"Now, anyone else with love problems we can solve?" asked Josh.

"Josh, I don't think you're the one to solve love problems. With you, Josh, it's love 'em, and leave 'em, and often I don't think you love 'em. It's more like, screw 'em, and leave 'em." The speaker was Eddie Burns, a tall, stoop- shouldered, dour looking young man. He was known for his often- cynical comments about life, and especially relationships. His father had died young from complications of alcoholism, and his mother was left the arduous task of raising two sons on her own. Eddie had joined the Air Force as a boy apprentice, and was in his sixth year of a ten-year engagement. He liked Jerome, and enjoyed their discussions, and often sought Jerome's opinion on different issues.

Josh looked at Eddie, and smiling sheepishly, said, "I make them happy, Eddie."

"No Josh, it's the money that makes them happy, not the sex."

"Well, you may be right there. It's a hell of a way to earn a living," Josh conceded.

"It is, and all these baby-face airmen and soldiers, away from home for the first time in their lives are madly sowing their wild oats with Singapore whores. Then they'll go back home and boast to their cronies about their sexual exploits with native women. They'll make it sound exotic." There was contempt in Eddie's voice.

"Do you really think they'll do that?" asked Josh.

"Wouldn't surprise me. What should happen though is every time one of these philanderers contracts gonorrhea or syphilis a letter should be sent to the parents." 'Dear Mr. and Mrs. Smith, we regret to inform you that your son, James, has contracted a venereal disease. He has been treated, and we expect him to make a full recovery, and do not think there will be a reoccurrence. However, please ensure he visits a doctor as soon as he returns home. Signed by the chief medical officer.' "Imagine their horror." 'Our son has that horrible disease, and after we told him to be so careful?' "Careful of what? Crossing the street? Parents don't talk with their children about sex. It's a taboo subject." Eddie stopped suddenly. He looked at the others who were listening intently to his diatribe. "Sorry guys. I'm on a roll. I'd better stop."

"Just as it was getting really interesting," said Geordie. "What parents should tell their children about sex."

"And what did yours tell you, Geordie?" asked Eddie.

"Nothing."

"My mother talked to me shortly before leaving," said Jerome. "I remember, she told me never to buy sex.' You can pay a terrible price physically,'" she said. "I thought about what happened to one of my favourite composers, Scott Joplin. I played some of his Rags for you the other night. A single encounter with a prostitute early in his life, years later cost him his marriage, his career, and all too prematurely, his life. He was dead at age forty-nine." The silence that followed was almost somber, as though each one in the group was contemplating his own behaviour and values. Josh broke the silence with a question for Jerome.

"Do you think Rebecca's mother thought you were in the relationship for the money? You know, the big dowry? Isn't that the procedure when the daughter of wealthy parents marries?"

"I don't think so Josh," replied Jerome. "Rebecca's father and I got along well. He was impressed with my going to university, and that I had specific goals. He knew I was a very independent minded person. No, the mother was definitely the stumbling block."

"Jerome, I didn't know you're going to university." Geordie was genuinely surprised. "All this time I've worked with you, and you've never mentioned university. Which university, may I ask?"

"Cambridge."

"Cambridge! You've got to be a genius to go there."

"Not quite, otherwise I wouldn't be going."

"Doesn't it cost a lot to go there?" asked Josh.

"It does, but fortunately I won a scholarship."

"Oh boy, it gets better. Cambridge, and on a scholarship," said Geordie. "Now you're being modest."

"Now you're being modest. And how come you're not an officer? Anyone who's won a scholarship to Cambridge should be an officer."

"It was an option, but then it meant purchasing special dress uniforms for dining- in nights, and running up mess fees. I really didn't want that. I thought, this isn't going to be my career. I don't need this. Then I imagined some former public school type asking me what school I went to, and what my father did, and again I thought, I don't need this. So here I am, senior aircraftsman, air radar." He looked at Geordie and smiled.

"One of the boys for now," said Geordie, "but when you get out you'll be going places."

"What will you study at Cambridge?" asked Josh.

"Mathematics."

Josh whistle softly. "That's beyond me," he said, and he looked admiringly at Jerome.

"This has all been very interesting," said Eddie, "but I'm tired, and I'm going to bed. Good night everyone." There was a chorus of "Good nights" as Eddie wandered down to his bed at the other end of the floor. Soon silence fell upon the second floor, and the sounds and fragrance of a tropical night wafted through Block 124.

"Mother, I can't understand why Jerome hasn't written. It has to be ten weeks since he arrived in Singapore, and not even a post card." Rebecca was clearly disappointed. "And he said he would write every week."

"Well dear, he's a long way from home, and sometimes young men do strange things."

"Such as?" asked Rebecca.

"It wouldn't surprise me, but he's become infatuated with a young native woman. They can be very seductive you know."

"Not Jerome," said Rebecca emphatically.

"Rebecca dear, he's away from the influence of home and close friends, and the men he's with will most probably encourage such an association. Native women are strangely appealing to white men. My dear, there's much evidence to support what I'm saying," replied Rebecca's mother. The tone of her voice was decidedly sympathetic.

"No mother, that's not Jerome. He's such a moral person."

"It's easy to be a moral person at home, and around close friends, but away from home and friends it's easy to yield to temptations, and there'll be plenty where Jerome is," Rebecca's mother replied quietly. "I think the real Jerome is showing up. Rebecca dear, he had to behave with you. He did, didn't he dear?" Suddenly, she was very anxious.

"Of course mother, Jerome was always the perfect gentleman," replied Rebecca, a hint of anger in her voice.

"Well," Rebecca's mother paused, uncertain what to say. Then suddenly, looking embarrassed, she said, "Well dear, some young men like to, er, well, sow their wild oats." For her to say such a thing was not easy. She was uncomfortable talking about sex, and did so in evasive terms. "Rebecca," she continued, "Jerome's a young man, and I'm sure he has strong desires like most men his age. That's the nature of men. Here, he had to control them. Not so in Singapore."

By now, Rebecca looked decidedly bewildered. "You really think Jerome would do that, mother?" Her eyes began to fill with tears.

"Oh, Rebecca dear," sighed her mother, her voice full of compassion, "You're so innocent, so vulnerable and easily hurt. I think this would be a good time to end this relationship, darling." She put her arms around Rebecca, and held her close while she sobbed.

"I loved him so much, mother, and I trusted him," Rebecca sobbed.

"I'm so sorry for you darling, but you know dear, you can expect this kind of behaviour of someone from his social class."

"You really believe class has anything to do with this?"

"Yes my dear, most certainly." Her mother's response was firm. "He's had all the benefits of your friendship. Now he's enjoying the friendship of another young woman, and I'm sure there'll be others, because, you know, one day he'll leave Singapore, and he'll have had his fun." There was a touch of bitterness in Mrs. Millden's voice.

"Maybe you're right mother," said Rebecca quietly. At sixteen it was difficult to believe someone could be so deceitful.

"Rebecca, my dear," her mother said in a soft voice, "you'll meet someone else. Someone from your social class who will love you for who you are."

Rebecca smiled weakly. "Thank you mother." Then she walked away to the quiet of her bedroom and wept.

~

Ten thousand miles away, Jerome leaned against the balcony wall of the second floor of Block 124, and looked down at the empty clay courts. Ten weeks since his arrival in Singapore, and nothing from Rebecca. He knew his letters must have reached her home, but obviously she wasn't reading them. Mother made sure of that, he was certain. Would Rebecca believe he had not bothered to write? Could she really be convinced some lovely, beguiling young native woman had won his affections? He believed Mrs. Millden could make a very convincing case. With no letters, Rebecca would hardly wait fourteen months for him. Mrs. Millden, it seemed, had won the day. Jerome could see the smug smile on her face. No daughter of hers was going to marry a bus driver's son.

"Penny for them, Jerome." Josh walked quietly to his side. "Just thinking about last night's conversation, and losing a girl friend."

"Maybe you'll find one in Singapore," suggested Josh.

"Well, right now I'm going to get ready to go into Singapore, and I might even look for a beautiful lady."

"Just don't go looking in Bugis Street," said Josh with a chuckle.

"Are you kidding? There are no beautiful women on Bugis Street. I walked through it last night before boarding the Changi bus. Depressing."

Josh laughed. "But the guys keep going."

"I'm off to the Art Museum. It's worth another visit.   Why don't you join me? I'll pay the fares."

"Thanks, but I'll stay here and read a little. Might go to the beach later. Enjoy your day, and beware of beautiful ladies."

Jerome selected his clothes carefully, as though he were going on a date. A short-sleeve, buff coloured shirt went well with his tan linen slacks, and brown, moccasin type casual shoes completed his ensemble. He looked every bit a Singapore resident. Shortly after eight-thirty he was on a bus for Singapore.

He saw her in profile, her thick black hair perfectly shaped around her neck. What so impressed Jerome was the perfection of her profile. She must have been aware of someone observing her. She turned, looked at Jerome, and smiled. Long, black lashes emphasized the darkness of her almond- shaped eyes. Jerome was a little embarrassed, and stammered, "Er, I was looking at the painting too. I just wondered what about this painting interests you? That is, I assume you are interested?"

"As a matter of fact, I am," she replied, still smiling at Jerome. "It's the whole composition. There's a wonderful balance in this painting, and the artist has blended the colours so effectively."

"You're obviously a true connoisseur of art."

"I don't know about being a connoisseur, though I do appreciate art."

Jerome thought her smile warm and appealing.

"May I invite you for a coffee?"

"Well now, I might just accept your invitation. Where had you in mind?"

"There's a great little coffee shop not far from here."

"A favourite of yours?"

"It's become one?"

She rose from the bench, and joined Jerome. Together they walked slowly, and quietly out of the Art Museum. Jerome noticed she walked with the practiced elegance of a model, and he wondered if she was one.

On the way to the coffee shop, Jerome introduced himself. "By the way, I'm Jerome, Jerome Callaghan."

"Well hello Jerome, I'm Francine Van Dyke, and I should say, I'm pleased to meet you." She smiled at Jerome, and her eyes sparkled.

Totally infatuated, Jerome returned Francine's smile. "I'm delighted to meet you."

"Tell me Jerome, do you work in Singapore?"

"No. I work in Changi.

"Ah, you're at the air base. You're with the Air Force."

"Yes. I'm here on behalf of His Majesty, King George V1."

"How long have you been here?"

"I arrived in Singapore on December 22, 1948."

"Just in time for Christmas."

"Yes. It wasn't the most memorable."

"You must be one of those who have been conscripted?"

"You're right. Two years in His Majesty's service. But thankfully, most of it will be here in Singapore."

By now they had reached the coffee shop, and entering, they seated themselves at a window seat.

"Latte, Francine?"

"Thank you. I will."

"And would you like a sandwich. They make a delicious toasted shrimp sandwich."

"I will share one with you, if you don't mind."

"That's fine. They're quite big."

Jerome gave his order, and returned to their conversation.

"Jerome, I'm interested in why you're thankful to be in Singapore."

"Oh, military life is so much better here than in England. It offers so much more than some dismal base back in England. Here there's much more freedom of movement. I caught a bus in Changi Village at 8.30 this morning. No checking out. No filling out a pass. Provided I'm back for work on Monday morning, no one cares. But I love being here. I like the climate. The flowers and vegetation are beautiful. It rains heavily at times, but then it soon dries, and it's always warm, and flowers are always blooming." Jerome paused. "I'm doing all the talking. Tell me something about yourself."

"That's all right. I'm interested in what you have to say. I hear that so many of these young men can't wait to return home. Your attitude is commendable." Francine sipped her latte, while Jerome bit into his sandwich.

"That's perfectly true. They simply don't appreciate this opportunity. They'll go home, get a job in their hometown, marry a hometown girl, and spend the rest of their lives there. And Singapore will become a distant memory."

"You sound a little annoyed."

"I'm annoyed at their provincialism. They don't see further than their hometown, or the shire they live in. They're so insular. But enough about these recruits. I want to hear something about you, Francine."

"Well, there isn't much to tell. I was born in Singapore, and lived here until June 1941, when my father sent my mother and me to live with his brother in Sydney, Australia. Father watched the advances by the Japanese army closely, and for our safety sent us to Australia. He joined us four months later. Sydney was home for the next four years. I attended college for two years when we returned to Singapore, and in August 1947 my father sent me to California for a year. I stayed with an aunt in San Mateo, and studied mostly art and art appreciation. It was a wonderful year. My aunt and her husband took me as far north as Seattle. We visited the art communities in Carmel and Tahoe. The year went all too quickly. I'd love to go again. I've suggested to my father that we go there for a vacation next year. He was very receptive of my suggestion. That's my story." Francine smiled at Jerome.

"Did you enjoy the years in Australia?"

"Very much so. It's a beautiful country, especially the east coast. I spent a lot of time in the Blue Mountains hiking. My favourite beach was Coffs Harbour, some 300 miles north of Sydney, miles of golden sand. We spent many days there during my school vacations. My father was so good about taking us places. I think he intended for us to see as much of the eastern states as possible. Quite honestly, I think I could have remained in Australia, but father wanted to return to Singapore. He believed there would be opportunities for him, and he was right."

"Obviously, your father has done well in business here."

"Yes, he has." Francine's response was quite emphatic. "Tell me, Jerome, what will you do when you return home?"

"I'll miss the warmth and colours of Singapore."

"Now I'm sure that's not all you'll do."

"I'll enter university, and study mathematics."

"Oh." Francine raised her eyebrows approvingly. "What university?"

"Cambridge."

"You must be very good at math."

"I won a scholarship, which helps considerably."

"You must be a very good student to win a scholarship to Cambridge, Jerome."

"Well, yes. I'm fortunate in that I enjoy the subject, and I spent hours studying."

"And when you finish at Cambridge, what then?"

"I hope to immigrate to America."

"Oh. Why America?" Francine showed surprise.

"Greater opportunities. England's such a closed society. So class conscious. Still so much depends on what school you went to, and what your father does, though I admit, the situation is improving."

Their conversation had continued for almost two hours, when Francine looked at her watch, and said, "Jerome, thank you for a most interesting afternoon, but I must go. I've a few things to do for tomorrow."

"I'll see you again, I hope." There was a sense of appeal in Jerome's request.

Francine seemed to hesitate before replying. "I'll give you my telephone number. You may call between six and nine in the evening." She handed Jerome a small piece of paper on which she had written her number.

"Thank you. I'll call you sometime during the week."

"No girl friend in England?"

"No, Francine. That's a story for another time." Jerome smiled at her.

"I look forward to hearing all about it. Goodbye, Jerome." She rose, and quickly left the café. Jerome stood and watched her disappear down Bras Basah Road. He felt the same feeling he had experienced all those months ago when he was with Rebecca. I wonder what Mrs. Van Dyke is like, he thought. He sat down, and ordered another latte.

The next evening, shortly after seven, Jerome phoned Francine. She answered.

"Well, Jerome, you don't waste any time."

"I didn't want you to think I had forgotten you."

"I hardly think you would do that."

"May I meet you for lunch on Saturday. If you like Indian food, I know a very nice Indian restaurant on Orchard Road."

"Why don't you call me on Thursday evening about the same time, and I'll give you an answer."

"Expect a call Francine. No is not an option."

"I shall have to consider that. In the meantime, enjoy the rest of the week. Good night Jerome."

"Good night, Francine." Jerome hung up the receiver slowly. He had wanted to talk more.

At seven o'clock Thursday evening, Jerome phoned Francine.

"Good evening, Jerome. You are so punctual."

"Now how did you know it was I?"

"Simple, Jerome. I was not expecting a call from anyone except you."

"Now that surprises me."

"I'm not a very social person. I go many places on my own."

"So I was rather privileged when you accepted my invitation for coffee."

"I suppose you could say that."

"Am I about to make it two in a row?"

"In a sense, yes. My parents would like to meet you, and so you are invited to my home for lunch on Saturday."

"I guess, really I have no option but to accept."

"Remember, no is not an option." Francine laughed softly.

"Do I need to be briefed before meeting your parents?"

"You'll love them. Incidently, my father and I will drive to the corner of Bukit Timah Road and Kampong Java Road at 12.30. We'll be in a black, 1948 Rover."

"Thank you very much. I shall be there. Until Saturday then, goodbye Francine."

"Good bye, Jerome. Look forward to seeing you on Saturday."

Jerome bought a coffee at the N.A.A.F.I. and walked slowly back to the barracks. Surely, there can't be another Mrs. Millden?

Jerome thought. Something told him this would be different. He went upstairs to the second floor, and sauntered along the wide balcony. Josh greeted him.

"Jerome. How would you like to accompany me into Singapore on Saturday? We could have lunch somewhere, and take in a movie."

"Josh, I would love to, but I've just accepted an invitation to lunch on that day. Maybe next Saturday."

"OK. But don't tell me you've met a beautiful lady, and you haven't told me about her?"

"Well, actually, I have, and her parents want to meet me, hence, the luncheon invitation. It's a little unnerving."

"And where did you meet this lady?"

"In the Art Museum, last weekend. Remember, I invited you"

"Oh, yes, I do. And you never told me a thing."

"Well, I had her phone number, and I didn't know if she would want to see me again. I thought she might have second thoughts. It's not as though I'm an officer."

"Jerome, what's that got to do with it? Cambridge bound, fabulous pianist, super personality. What more could she want?"

"Oh, Josh, you're biased."

"Well, you enjoy your luncheon date. I'll still go in."

"Josh. Make it lunch and a movie."

He looked at Jerome, and smiled. "I promise. Now I'm going to get an early night. Good night, Jerome. See you for breakfast."

"Good night, Josh."

Jerome was at the corner of Bukit Timah Road, and Kampong Java Road by 12.15. Five minutes later, Mr. Van Dyke drove up in a sleek black Rover, with Francine beside him. She stepped out onto the pavement, and greeted Jerome. The driver's door opened, and Mr. Van Dyke stretched out a long leg, slowly emerged from the car, and rose to his full height. A slight stoop lowered his more than six feet. Casually dressed in light linen clothing, he walked around the front of the car toward Jerome.

"Daddy, I'd like you to meet Jerome."

He reached out a big hand, which Jerome clasped.

"Hello, Jerome, I'm very pleased to meet you. But Francine, you didn't tell us Jerome is so tall." Mr. Van Dyke laughed heartily, and Jerome smiled.

"I'm so use to being in the same house as you, daddy."

"Yes, but I'm looking up at this young man."

"Nevertheless sir, I'm delighted to meet you."

"Please, Mr. Van Dyke, Jerome. Well now, let's go and enjoy lunch," and opening a rear door, he beckoned Jerome to a seat. He slid easily onto the leather seat. Very quickly they were on their way.

"So Jerome, Francine tells me you are enjoying Singapore."

"Very much, Mr. Van Dyke. I'd almost like to stay here."

"Well you know, I could arrange that, but then Francine tells us you have a scholarship to Cambridge University. Don't give that up."

"Oh, no, I'd never do that. It's the ticket to my future."

"Now that sounds most interesting. I'll have to ask you more about that later."

Francine turned around, and looked at Jerome." You must have made good connections."

"I did, but to be sure, I caught an early bus out of Changi."

"Was it crowded?"

"No. Surprisingly quiet. I actually dozed for some of the time."

Francine smiled at Jerome, and there was gentleness in her eyes.

Soon the car passed through a wide gateway, and stopped on a large graveled area before a sprawling bungalow, set amidst lush, manicured lawns decorated with exotic looking flowerbeds. A deep verandah ran the width of the house. Jerome stepped out of the car, and paused before climbing the wide steps to the verandah. He looked at the spacious lawns, and the colourful flowers, and thought of his little home in Eldon with its tiny, bleak, flag-stoned back yard sandwiched between the neighbours' high wooden fences.

Mr Van Dyke noticed Jerome scrutinizing the garden. "Do you have a garden back home, Jerome?"

"No. Nothing but a tiny, empty back yard, and the pavement is our front garden." Jerome didn't even turn round.

"That's sad, Jerome. Everyone should have a garden with flowers. They give such joy."

Jerome turned, and looked at Mr. Van Dyke. "Someone else once said something like to me. He created beauty."

"And he most probably was at peace with himself."

"Yes, as a matter of fact, he was."

Jerome looked at Francine's father, and smiled wistfully. Just yesterday he had received a letter from his mother with the sad news that John Trewethey was dead. He had died on March 5th following a stroke. He was sixty-three. The funeral was two days ago. Hundreds would have attended. Jerome had sent John the promised cards, and he was delighted. Now Jerome recalled a tall, slightly stooped man, his broad-brimmed hat shading his tanned, creased face, waving goodbye. That was a final farewell.

Jerome walked slowly toward the broad steps leading to the verandah. He looked up to see a strikingly attractive lady of medium height standing at the top of the steps. He realized instantly from whom Francine had inherited her looks. As Jerome drew close to her, she greeted him.

"Hello, Jerome. I'm Francine's mother. Welcome to our home." She took Jerome's outstretched hand in both of hers, and smiled at him.

"Good afternoon, Mrs. Van Dyke. Thank you so much for inviting me. I was just admiring your beautiful garden."

"Why, thank you Jerome. We derive much pleasure from it."

"My dear, Jerome tells me he does not have a garden in England. And I thought all English homes had a garden."

"Mr. Van Dyke, there are too many that do not."

Mrs. Van Dyke turned to Francine. "My dear, you didn't say you had met such a handsome young man." Jerome blushed.

"Mother, you're embarrassing Jerome."

Mrs. Van Dyke took Jerome's arm, and ushered him into the house. Already he liked this lady, and was feeling very relaxed. Her manner was sincere, and she gave Jerome the impression of wanting others to enjoy her home. It was not a symbol of achievement, but a place to share with others, and Jerome was about to do that.

"Now Francine, my dear, perhaps Jerome would like to wash his hands before lunch."

"As a matter of fact, I would."

"Let me show you to the bathroom, Jerome."

"Thank you, Francine."

She led him to a room just beyond the tiled entrance hall. Jerome soaked his hands, and splashed water over his face. After the bus rides, this was refreshing. When he returned to the front room, Mrs. Van Dyke asked everyone to go to the dining room for lunch.

"Jerome, you will sit to my right, and Francine will sit opposite you."

"Thank you," said Jerome, and he waited until Mrs. Van Dyke was seated before sitting down. This was not lost on Mrs. Van Dyke.

～

The lunch was a gastronomic delight, and the conversation flowed as easily as did the wine.

"Jerome, Francine told me you enjoy prawns, and so I had Misha, our cook, prepare these king prawns in a curried sauce."

"Why, how kind of you, Mrs. Van Dyke. They look delicious."

"Curried dishes must be something new for you, Jerome," said Mr. Van Dyke.

"Oh, yes. You know, to be quite honest, food in England is rather bland, and that's so true of food at the base. Military cooks can't boil water."

Mr. Van Dyke was smiling at Jerome. "The food is that bad?"

"It really is."

"Well, Jerome," said Francine, "I think you'll enjoy Misha's cooking. She's been with us for years, and we've yet to taste a poor meal."

"Oh, she's marvelous," said Francine's mother, enthusiastically. "We're so blessed to have her. So, Jerome, eat heartily."

"Thank you, Mrs. Van Dyke."

"I think mother wants to see you put weight on your bones, Jerome," said Francine, with a smile.

"Pay no heed to Francine, Jerome. I simply want you to eat well."

"Now, Jerome, good food requires good wine, and I see your glass is almost empty." Mr. Van Dyke was holding a bottle of Hunter Valley Riesling in his hand.

"Thank you. A little," and Jerome held out his glass. "I have to admit, wine with my lunch is a new experience."

"You wouldn't have it any other way, would you father?"

"Of course not, Francine." He smiled at her, and then, looking at Jerome, he rose, and said, "I would like to propose a toast to our young guest. To Jerome, may he succeed in all his endeavours."

Mrs. Van Dyke and Francine raised their glasses, and in unison, said, "To Jerome."

He sat in speechless surprise. Then, looking at each in turn, he said," I've never been toasted before. Thank you so much. I feel quite honoured."

Then, with an impish smile on her face, Francine looked at Jerome, "Now the interrogation begins," she said.

Initially, Jerome looked a little stunned, but Francine's mother intervened. "Jerome, disregard that remark, Francine is being most discourteous."

"Mother, really, you said, 'I have so many questions to ask this young man of yours.'"

"But my dear, asking questions is hardly an interrogation."

"Mm, I'll reserve judgment on that."

"My dear, you're quite incorrigible." Mrs. Van Dyke's laughter was subdued.

Jerome entered into the humour of the situation. "Am I allowed to refrain from answering questions?"

"Only the most trivial," replied Francine, smiling, "and believe me, there are none."

"First, I think Jerome needs his wine glass filling." Before Jerome could refuse, Mr. Van Dyke had reached over, and filled his glass.

"And I thought this was a luncheon invitation," said Jerome quietly, as mother, father, and daughter erupted into laughter. Blushing slightly, Jerome dropped his face into his hands. "I'm going to have to get use to this Van Dyke humour."

"First question," said Francine with a smile. Then her mother addressed Jerome in a slightly more serious voice.

"Jerome, since it is obvious you wish to date our daughter, we simply would like to know a little about you."

"Why, of course. I know my parents will do the same when some young man begins to date my sister."

"Well then, this is no surprise."

"Mr. and Mrs. Van Dyke, I was expecting this. Indeed, I would have been surprised had you not asked about my background." Jerome looked at them expectantly. "There isn't much to tell. I've been out of school less than a year, and until being shipped out to Singapore with His Majesty's forces, I lived at home with my parents, and younger sister and brother."

"But Jerome," said Mrs. Van Dyke, "Francine tells us you have a scholarship to Cambridge University, and one has to be very clever to win a scholarship to that university."

"I'm fortunate in that I enjoy math, and I study hard. I also see education as the key to my future."

"Ah, Jerome, that's what I wanted to ask you about. You made that same remark in the car."

Jerome looked first at Mr. Van Dyke, and then at Mrs. Van Dyke. "I will be the first Callaghan to attend university. All my relatives, especially on the Callaghan side, will be watching my progress. I intend to do well. Success at university can spell success for me in a career."

"Your attitude is most commendable, and I'm sure you will be successful," said Francine's mother. "But Francine also tells us you intend to immigrate to America after you graduate."

"Yes, that is my intention. There just seem to be greater opportunities in that country."

"What part of America will you go to, Jerome?" Francine's father was looking intently at Jerome.

"The Northwest. Washington State, and most probably Seattle."

"That's very specific, Jerome," replied Mr. Van Dyke.

"I've always been fascinated by America, and I can recall poring over maps of the different states. Oregon and Washington in particular interested me. But I have a further reason. I'm interested in actuarial science, and major insurance companies in the Seattle area are often looking for graduates with such a background. I also believe I can study for my Master's Degree while employed. Something I would also like to do."

Mr. Van Dyke had pushed his chair back from the table, and was watching Jerome intently. "Jerome, I admire someone who has plans for his future, and knows where he is going, and you, young man, are such a person. I like that." A smile lit up his face, and he nodded approvingly.

"You know, when you've finished university, I think I could find a place for you in my business." He laughed, but it was not in jest.

"Jerome," asked Francine, "Do you think you'd like living in Singapore?"

"Yes, I think I would, but I'd like to try America first. I think there's so much I'd enjoy—the size, the mountains, the ocean, and the forests. I'd also like to learn to ski."

"Now that's something you could never learn here," said Francine, laughing.

"But your family will miss you if you leave," said Francine's mother in a soft voice, and a sadness in her eyes.

"That's true, Mrs. Van Dyke."

"But you have a sister and a brother at home, so they will be good company for your parents. She will not lose all her babes." She smiled warmly at Jerome.

"Just one." Jerome returned the smile.

"If Francine were to go away, we would miss her greatly. She is all we have." Mrs. Van Dyke looked at her daughter with tears in her eyes.

"I think I can understand how you would feel." For a moment, Jerome felt uncomfortable, though he felt Mrs. Van Dyke was preparing for the inevitable. Her husband looked on in silence.

"But Jerome," began Mrs. Van Dyke, "you're a very good student. I want to know if you do anything else outside of your studies?"

"My dear," interrupted her husband, "I would think Jerome is busy enough with his studies."

"Well, that's almost true, Mr. Van Dyke, though I do play the piano a little."

"Why then, Jerome, you must play for us," said Mrs. Van Dyke enthusiastically.

Francine intervened. "Mother, perhaps Jerome does not prefer an audience."

"An audience of three? Would you rather not, Jerome?"

"The truth is, I would love to play your baby grand. I've been quietly admiring it."

"Perhaps a little Beethoven?" Mrs. Van Dyke smiled at Jerome.

"My dear, that's asking rather a lot," said Mr. Van Dyke.

"Oh, we'll let Jerome decide," she replied.

"Twinkle, twinkle," said Jerome, quietly.

Francine laughed. "The Mozart version."

Jerome waited for Francine's parents to rise from the table. Then he rose, and walked slowly to the piano. He lifted the lid of the key- board, and raised the big covering of the sound- board. Francine's mother watched Jerome's deliberate movements intently. She began to anticipate something quite beautiful. "Jerome, would you like some music?" It was a sincere question.

"Thank you, that wont be necessary."

He sat down, and adjusted the piano bench. For a moment, there was an intense silence in the room. Jerome turned, and looking at Mrs. Van Dyke, he said quietly, "The second movement from The Pathetique." She nodded, and smiled, as Jerome began playing the beautiful slow movement. She knew they were in for something special, as soon as his long, supple fingers began moving over the key- board. Soon, she had closed her eyes, and was totally absorbed in the music. As she listened, she knew Francine had found the man of her dreams, and she had lost a daughter. For a moment, she opened her eyes, and looked at Francine. It was inevitable. She had always known that one day Francine would meet someone who would take Francine out of her life. Ever so smoothly, Jerome began the joyful Fur Elisle, and continued with a medley of Beethoven piano pieces that included the 'Moonlight Sonata, and the Apassionata. As always, the music possessed him. At one moment he lifted his head, eyes closed, then he would drop his head as though listening intently to the music. This was Beethoven, and Jerome had great compassion for this genius, whose deafness had so tormented him. "Just think," he would say, "Beethoven heard, though he was deaf, and what he heard was beautiful, and he gave it to the world."

When finally he stopped, Mr. Van Dyke said excitedly, "My goodness, Jerome, are you sure you're not going to be a concert pianist?"

"No, though at seventeen I became the youngest Fellow of the Royal Schools of Music. The adjudicators suggested I consider the concert stage."

"Oh, Jerome," sighed Mrs. Van Dyke, "That was beautiful, and you, my dear young man, are very talented."

"Jerome, what other talents are you keeping from us?" asked Francine.

Her mother looked at her, and asked, "My dear, where did you find this young man?"

"Actually mother, I didn't find him, he found me."

"Francine, my dear, you expect me to believe that." Her mother smiled at her.

"She's telling the truth, Mrs. Van Dyke. I became more fascinated with your daughter, than with the painting we were looking at. I began to admire Francine more than I did the painting, and here I am."

"Well Jerome, if I may express a personal opinion, I think you have very good taste." Mr. Van Dyke and Francine joined in the laughter that filled the room. Jerome blushed a little, and smiled. Before leaving, he played Chopin's Waltz in C, at Mrs. Van Dyke's request. She hugged him before he left, and he thanked her for the delicious food, but especially for her hospitality.

"Thank you, for making me feel so at home. This has been a wonderful afternoon for me."

"My dear Jerome," said Mrs. Van Dyke, "you have provided us such beautiful entertainment. It's a long time since I have heard Beethoven played so well on our piano. You realize you shall have to come again."

"To play Beethoven, or see me, mother?" said Francine, a smile on her face.

"Why both, my dear, of course." Her mother was still smiling.

Jerome said goodbye to Francine and her mother, and Mr. Van Dyke drove him to the bus stop.

"Thank you for the ride, Mr. Van Dyke."

"You're welcome, Jerome. You must come again." He shook hands warmly with Jerome, and drove off.

Jerome was left to the waning light of a late tropical afternoon, and its delicious fragrances. The afternoon had been like no other.

Back in the Van Dyke home, Mrs. Van Dyke looked at her daughter, and in a soft voice said, "He is a good man, Francine. You are fortunate to have met one such as he, but then, my dear, he also is fortunate."

"Thank you mother, and thank you for making him so welcome."

Walking over to her mother, she embraced her. "I love you."

"And I love you, my dear. I think I'll walk in the garden before it gets dark."

"And I'll play a little Mozart, but don't expect a Jerome performance," said Francine smiling, as she sat down at the piano.

"I'll be listening, dear."

The day after the luncheon, Jerome knew it was time to inform his parents about Francine and her parents. He had been in love once before, but this time there was a difference. This time there was a mother who approved of the relationship. This time there was a mother who had held his hand warmly, as she welcomed him into her home. This time there was a mother who did not concern herself with where he lived, or what his father did. This time there was a mother who liked him for whom he was. He was nineteen, and very much in love with a woman two years older than he, but marriage was at least four years away, and for three of those four years they would be apart. This time though, he knew the addressee would read his letters. This love could be a distraction as well as a motivation.

He was sitting at his low locker, using the top as a desk. At seven in the evening, the floor was very quiet. Suddenly, Josh was standing beside him.

"Writing home?"

"Yes Josh. I'm breaking the news about Francine."

"How do you think your parents will receive that?"

"Mum will love it. Dad will remind me about three years at university. He doesn't want anything to interfere with that. I agree. University is top priority."

"I can understand his being anxious for you not to blow such an opportunity. Will Francine wait?"

"I really think so," replied Jerome, looking off into the distance. Then he looked at Josh. "She's that kind of a person. She's sincere. She'll share in my goals."

"Must be nice to have someone like that in your life. But you're so young, Jerome."

"Assuming we get married, I'll be twenty-three, and Francine will be twenty-five." Jerome seemed to ponder his reply.

"And you'll have the rest of your lives together. That could be a long time, Jerome." Josh laughed quietly.

"Yes it could, Josh, so it's important to build a strong relationship. There have to be shared values, and of course, our shared faith will be critical."

"You're fortunate to have that, Jerome. Don't forget to invite me to the wedding." Josh smiled.

"Absolutely, Josh. You'll receive one of the first invitations. Might even name a son after you."

"Then I would feel honoured. By the way, how was the lunch?"

"Great," replied Jerome with obvious enthusiasm. "Her parents are wonderful people. I felt so comfortable with them. Her mother is such a warm, generous person. How different from Rebecca's mother. No questions about what kind of a house I live in, or what my father does. I was so relieved. I'll be going there again. Incidentally Josh, they have the most beautiful baby grand."

"And guess who got to play it?"

"But by invitation."

"I bet they didn't want you to stop either."

"Now, how was the movie?"

"So, so. Humphrey Bogart in 'Knock on Any Door.' I like Bogart, but I don't think this was one of his better films. He's a lawyer in this one, and defends a boy from the slums, who robs a store, and in the process shoots and kills a policeman."

"So you don't recommend it?"

"No."

"We'll definitely take in a film together, Josh. Maybe this weekend."

"What about Francine?"

"I'll tell her it's my night out with the boys."

"Mm. I'm not so sure that's a good idea. I hardly want to come between you and a beautiful romance." Josh chuckled.

"How about this Friday? I just remember, Francine is going somewhere with her mother."

"OK. Friday night it is. Now I'll leave you to finish your letter. I think I'll go for a beer. See you later."

"Stay sober."

"I'd better, or I wont have enough for the show on Friday."

Jerome watched Josh saunter toward the stairs, and then he turned to the task of completing his letter. After all, it was a most significant one. He began: "I have to tell you I have met a lovely young lady. Her name is Francine Van Dyke. I've enclosed a photograph of her . . ."

One day in early April, Jerome asked Josh if he would like to go to a symphony concert. There was going to be one late in May, and the guest soloist was the celebrated pianist, Solomon. Singapore was one stop on his world tour.

"Jerome, I've never been to a concert, but having listened to you play, I think I might enjoy one."

"Good. Then be my guest. I'll get the tickets."

"Well, thank you. Perhaps you can brief me about some of the music," Josh grinned.

"OK. I'll tell you something about the Beethoven piano concerto."

"I assume Francine will be going?"

"She's getting the tickets."

Josh's acceptance was to profoundly change his life. Not only was the concert to be a first, so also was love.

Anne Leung met Francine at a fund-raising bazaar for the Singapore Symphony Orchestra. Both were admiring a copy of an Ansel Adams' photograph. Anne bought the copy, and then the two of them went out for a coffee. They quickly discovered that one thing they shared was a love of music. Anne played flute with the Singapore Symphony Orchestra; Francine confessed a failed aspiration to becoming a concert pianist. After this initial meeting, their friendship blossomed, and rarely a week passed, but they did something together. Now Anne, excited about the forthcoming concert, had obtained three tickets for Francine, who had suggested they meet after the concert.

"Well Jerome, do I look presentable?"

Josh stood before Jerome. He was elegantly dressed in a tan-coloured, tailored linen suit. Ivory cuff links fastened the French cuffs of his cream shantung shirt. His soft blue tie had a perfectly symmetrical Windsor knot. For a moment, Jerome stood speechless.

"Wow! Are we going to a Command Performance? Josh, you look like something out of Saville Row. Do you mind if I walk a few paces behind you?"

Jerome's approval brought a broad smile to Josh's face.

"I think I'll allow you to walk beside me."

"If I didn't know, I'd swear you had a date, Josh."

"Well, we are meeting Francine."

"You know, I'm beginning to have second thoughts about going," said Jerome, with a perfectly straight face.

"It's OK Jerome. I'm not going to Cambridge, and I don't play the piano like Solomon."

They laughed, and to some derisive comments from a few Squadron members present, the two of them went down the stairs, and out to a waiting taxi. The occasion warranted one.

The Victoria Theatre was packed. The concert was sold out. People who came hoping to buy tickets the night of the concert were disappointed. Solomon gave a brilliant performance, and after four standing ovations, proceeded to play three encores. The audience loved him, and Josh could not have experienced a better concert inauguration. He was visibly impressed with the audience's response. Jerome assured him Solomon's performance was worthy of the standing ovation. Chattering their approval, the people spilled noisily into the Singapore night, among them, Francine, Jerome, and Josh, looking for Anne. She appeared near the main entrance, holding her slim black flute case. Petite, and very attractive, she claimed her large, dark eyes were part of her Indian heritage on her mother's side. Long black hair cascaded over her shoulders, and swayed with her quick, short steps. She greeted Francine warmly with a hug.

"Anne, I would like you to meet Jerome and Josh. They're on the same squadron at Changi."

"Hello. I'm pleased to meet both of you. Francine has told me much about you, Jerome."

"Complimentary, I hope," Jerome was quick to interject.

"Why, of course," replied Anne. She looked at him with sparkling, dark eyes. "But I know nothing about Josh, so let's get something to eat; I'm hungry, and I can ask him all sorts of questions." She smiled at Josh, who reciprocated warmly.

Anne led them to a nearby restaurant frequented by orchestra members, and noted for its good food. Inside, they were shown to a corner table.

"Now Josh," began Anne, turning her attention to him. "I believe this was your first concert?"

"It was."

"So what did you like most about the concert?"

"I'd have to say it was the piano concerto, simply because Jerome prepared me for that piece. He told me what to listen for, and I enjoyed it."

"Oh, Jerome, you have a musical background"?

"Yes, I play the piano."

"And Jerome," interrupted Francine, "don't you dare say, 'a little.'"

Josh laughed. "Jerome is very secretive about his accomplishments."

"Well, I know he's going to Cambridge on a scholarship," said Anne.

"Now lets discuss Anne's flute playing," Jerome chuckled.

Just then a waiter came to their table requesting their order. They decided on a variety of tasty dishes that included Szechuan prawn hot pot, sliced beef with assorted vegetables, and sweet and sour boneless pork. The waiter moved away quietly, and conversation resumed.

"Josh," Anne asked, "do you think you'll go to another concert?"

"I'd like to, though I admit I'd want to listen to music I could whistle or hum after hearing it."

"Strauss or Mozart," said Anne. "You've probably whistled a Strauss tune without realizing it."

"That I don't know. I've got a lot of listening and learning to do."

"Did you have music in your home, when you were growing up?" Anne could not curb her curiosity.

"Not really. Neither of my parents played a musical instrument, and certainly my father showed no interest in music. When I was eleven, my mother died." There was sadness in his eyes.

Anne hesitated a moment. "Oh, how sad." There was a note of sympathy in her voice.

Josh continued. "I'd have to say, childhood was not the happiest time of my life."

Anne was beginning to feel a little uncomfortable, and Jerome eased the situation. "Knowing something of Josh's background, I think he's done remarkably well."

"Forgive me Josh, I'm being too personal," said Anne quietly."

"Not really, Anne. I guess most of us have painful memories." Josh looked at Anne, and smiled softly.

"But do keep music in your life. It's a wonderful antidote, and can be so restful."

"Yes, I can believe that. How long have you been playing the flute?"

"A long time. I started when I was four. During the occupation I played as often as I could, but it was difficult. I was always afraid of attracting the Japanese. Then in 1946, when the Symphony Orchestra resumed playing, I auditioned, and I was accepted. Oh, I was so excited."

"The occupation must have been a terrible time," said Josh.

"It was. We lived in constant fear. I lost two uncles. One died of a heart attack, the other was sent to Japan to work in a factory along with prisoners of war. After the war, we learned he had died of typhus. Apparently he was in terrible pain shortly before his death. Four years after the end of the war I still hate the Japanese. We Chinese cannot forget the horror of the massacre in Nanking. It will take a long time for me to forgive them." Anne became silent. When she looked at Josh there was a poignant sadness in her eyes. "Those are my painful memories, Josh."

"I can understand why you don't like talking about them," he replied quietly.

Francine intervened, and changed the subject. "Josh, Jerome tells me you enjoy Singapore."

"I do. I wish I could spend the balance of my time here, but I'm not allowed to."

"Would you like to return here to live?"

"If I could get a job I liked, I would."

"Any prospects?" asked Francine.

"I haven't enquired. In fact, I'm not sure where to start. Would you know?"

"Well, I could ask my father. What do you think, Jerome?" Francine placed her hand over Jerome's, and squeezing it gently, smiled at him.

"I'm sure he has many good contacts, darling. The one problem is Josh still has more than two years left on his Air Force contract."

"And there's no way out of it?" asked Francine.

"It is possible to purchase one's discharge, but I don't know what the conditions are. I guess I should enquire. And I appreciate your interest in my future, Francine," Josh chuckled.

"You're very welcome, Josh. I think we all can benefit from help at some time or other."

"Now I have a question for you. What do you do, Francine?"

"I'm a loans officer with the Bank of Singapore, and I also interview prospective employees. It's interesting work, and quite unrelated to what I studied in college."

"Which was?"

"Art and art history. The person who hired me must have thought I would make a suitable trainee. But this was shortly after the war, and banks were looking for young people with university or college education."

"So if I need a loan, you're the person I should see," said Josh with a broad grin.

"Actually, we do not make loans to military persons, just permanent residents of Singapore."

"I guess that makes sense. Imagine trying to get back a loan from some airman who's returned to England. Goodbye loan," Josh chuckled. "Did you meet Anne through the bank?"

"No. We met at a fund raiser for the Symphony Orchestra."

"That was more than two years ago," said Anne. "I saw her talking with an orchestra member, and I thought, now there's someone who looks to know something about music. I was most impolite. I just breezed into their conversation, and took over."

"Looking back, Anne, you really were."

"I just wanted to save you from lover boy. He was a notorious flirt."

"You mean he no longer is," asked Jerome.

"No," replied Anne. "He's actually married, and has a daughter. Any rate, Francine and I have been inseparable ever since. Well, until Jerome came on the scene." Anne smiled at Jerome. "No offence, Jerome."

"None taken."

"Now I know how you two met, but I don't know what you do, Anne."

"I'm a secretary. As such, I make appointments, answer the phone, and type."

"A secretary to whom?"

"The Commissioner of Police. He's a wonderful boss."

"You move in high places," said Jerome.

"On occasions," Anne quipped.

"Josh," said Jerome, "maybe you could be his personal mechanic."

"No such position," said Anne.

"Chauffeur?" suggested Jerome.

"No vacancy," Anne laughed.

Francine turned to Jerome. "My dear, I'm going to phone father to come and pick up Anne and me. It's getting late, and you two have to get a bus."

"How nice, a ride home. Thank you, Francine," said Anne.
Francine soon returned. Her father would be at the restaurant
in ten minutes. She looked at Jerome and Josh. " Well, gentlemen,
thank you for a wonderful evening. We'll have to do this again.
Maybe for your second concert, Josh."

"I think I would like that," "Josh replied with a warm smile."

"I want to add my thanks, too," said Anne. "It's been so nice
meeting the two of you."

"Thank you," said Josh. "The feeling is quite mutual." He
smiled at both Anne and Francine.

"It's been a great evening, and you're right, Francine, we'll
have to do this again, Josh's second concert or not," Jerome
concluded.

Jerome and Josh shared the bill, and the four of them walked
outside as Francine's father drove up. Jerome opened the rear
door, and Francine and Anne sat together.

"Good evening, Mr. Van Dyke."

"Good evening, Jerome. You young people have a good
evening?"

"Wonderful," replied Jerome. "Good night ladies."

Francine and Anne laughed, and returned the greeting.
"Good night, and thank you, gentlemen."

Jerome closed the door, and the car sped away into the
darkness of the Singapore night. Then turning to Josh, he said,
"Let's stay at the Y.M. tonight."

"Good idea. I wasn't looking forward to a bus ride to Changi
at this time of night, and one taxi ride's enough for one day." Josh
grinned at Jerome, "After all that food I need a walk, and I want
to thank you for inviting me to the concert, and paying for my
ticket."

"Josh, you're most welcome. I'm so pleased you enjoyed it."

"Francine is a beautiful lady."

"Thanks Josh. She has a character to match her beauty, too."

"I like Anne. She's a lot of fun," Josh added. "I'd like to see her
again."

"Well, Josh, I'll have to see what I can do about that," and placing a hand on Josh's shoulder, Jerome added, "that's what a friend should do, isn't it?"

"I think you're right, old chap," Josh replied with a grin. Then they began a leisurely stroll toward Orchard Road, and the Y.M. That night their friendship attained a new depth.

Jerome kept his word about Anne. With Francine as intercessor, he was able to put Josh in touch with Anne. Josh quickly took the initiative, and within a week of his initial phone call, he and Anne went out on their first date. In the months that followed, they met regularly. Hardly a weekend passed that they did not meet, and go somewhere. For Josh, this was a wonderful new experience, an almost giddy time. His past associations with women had been casual, mostly one night, affairs. Too often he had dressed early in the morning, and closed the bedroom door quietly behind him. In Singapore he had associated only with prostitutes, which had resulted in his first ever bout of syphilis. Fortunately, he was cured of this cruel disease, but the experience scared him. When he met Jerome, he began to learn the merits of a genuine relationship with a woman, and then he met Anne, and she was different. She won his love, and commanded his respect, and he relished every moment they were together. Shortly into their courtship, Anne invited Josh to her home to meet her parents, and have lunch with them. Anne was nervous. Her father harboured some resentment toward the British. He felt they had betrayed the people of Singapore. Poor leadership was to blame for the rapid, and total collapse of the Singapore defences in 1941. "The Japanese," he said, "outmanoeuvred the British." Certainly, the death of a brother in a Japanese armaments factory endeared him to neither the Japanese nor the British. However, having acknowledged the suffering by the British prisoners-of-war, he felt compassion for them, and by 1949 he had all but forgiven the British for their inept leadership.

Josh enjoyed the lunch, and Anne's parents enjoyed the company of the mannerly, witty young Englishman. "You must come again young man," said Anne's father, as Josh was leaving. Anne looked rather sternly at her father. "Daddy, his name is Josh."

"Oh, forgive me, daughter, I mean, Josh," and laughing excitedly, he shook Josh's hand vigorously.

On the Thursday after the lunch at Anne's, Josh phoned Anne.

"If you're free on Saturday, I'd like to meet you."

"Oh Josh, I'm so glad you phoned. I have something so exciting to tell you. I was talking to the Commissioner about you, and he's arranging for you to meet with the manager of the Harbour Police Maintenance Department." Anne was having difficulty containing her excitement.

"Wow!" You see what happens when you know people in high places."

"You get to meet the right people," replied Anne. "But I hope something comes of this."

"Can we talk more about this on Saturday?" asked Josh.

"Why, yes. Where shall we meet?"

"Outside that restaurant close to the Art Museum."

"What time?"

"Ten o'clock."

"Good. Ten o'clock it is. See you then, darling. I think by then, I'll have a phone number for you. Goodbye Josh."

"Goodbye Anne." With a smile, Josh hung up.

On Saturday, they met as arranged, and Anne had a phone number for Josh. He was to phone a Geoff Dawson anytime between 7.00p.m. and 9.00p.m. Josh ate a light breakfast, while Anne drank a latte. They talked about the upcoming interview. Anne was optimistic. She was convinced it would result in a job offer.

"I don't think the Commissioner would have contacted Mr. Dawson, if he didn't think there was the clear possibility of a job."

"Anne," said a rather skeptical Josh, "I hope you're right, otherwise an early discharge won't mean much."

"Darling, you have to be positive."

"You're sounding like Jerome," said Josh, and they both laughed.

Early in the afternoon, they went to a film. Then Josh walked Anne to her bus stop, and saw her onto the bus.

Shortly after seven o'clock the following evening, Josh phoned Geoff Dawson. On the phone, he was a man of few words. For him, conversations were face- to- face affairs.

"Is Saturday convenient for a meeting, Josh?'

"Yes sir."

"Good. Say ten o'clock at The Union Jack Club."

"I'll be there," said an excited Josh.

"See you then. Good night, Josh."

A slightly bewildered Josh hung up the phone. Certainly a man of few words, thought Josh, but I do have an interview.

At nine-thirty the following Saturday, Josh entered the lobby of The Union Jack Club. He sat in a comfortable rattan chair facing the entrance. At two minutes to ten, a man above medium height, slim, and darkly handsome, entered. His thick, black hair was immaculately groomed, and his clothing, tastefully selected, enhanced his appearance. Geoff Dawson believed managers should display a certain sartorial style. He walked up to Josh, who rose to meet him.

"Josh Quinn, I presume. I'm Geoff Dawson."

"I'm pleased to meet you Mr. Dawson."

"There's a nice restaurant near here. I suggest we go there," said Geoff Dawson.

"Very good. Sounds a little more comfortable than this lobby," replied Josh. Geoff Dawson smiled in approval.

"How long have you been in Singapore?"

"Almost three years."

"Always at Changi?"

"Yes. 205 Transport Squadron."

"You obviously like Singapore"

"Love it, "replied Josh.

"I gather you went through the fitter's course in England?"

"Yes I did, but because I had finished two years of an apprenticeship for internal combustion and diesel engines, the course was considerably shortened for me."

"Oh, you've had experience with diesel engines?" Geoff Dawson was interested.

"Yes, but I haven't worked on them for a while."

By now they had reached the restaurant. Obviously a regular, Geoff Dawson was greeted cordially, and shown to a corner table. Both ordered coffee. Josh added toast, and Geoff Dawson ordered a fruit platter.

At the end of more than an hour's conversation, Geoff Dawson had assured Josh of a job in a newly reorganized, and expanding Maintenance Department of the Harbour Police. The job would begin in September.

"I can hardly believe what I'm hearing," said an astonished Josh.

"Well Josh start believing, and get busy with that purchase of discharge."

"I certainly will"

"Keep me informed, and I hope to hear good news from you." Geoff Dawson was smiling as he shook hands with Josh. "I'll pay the bill on my way out."

"Thank you very much for everything, Mr. Dawson. I greatly appreciate all you've done for me."

"My pleasure Josh. I hope you'll be joining us in September. Enjoyed talking with you." He left money with the cashier, and walked out of the restaurant. Josh ordered another coffee, and pondered his considerable good fortune.

One Friday afternoon, shortly after work on the Squadron had finished for the day, Josh, wrapped only in a towel, wandered over to Jerome, who was sitting on his bed reading a letter from home.

"Jerome, take a shower after you've finished reading the letter, and get dressed. We're going into the village for dinner."

Jerome looked up from his letter. "We are? Your treat?" He smiled at Josh.

"If you like. I have something to discuss with you."

"Mm. Sounds serious."

"It is. That's why I want you to have dinner with me."

"OK, fifteen, twenty minutes?"

"That's good," replied Josh, and went off to shower.

Jerome undressed. His clothes were damp with sweat. Soon, he was enjoying a cool, refreshing shower He dressed in a pair of light, tan worsted slacks, a matching short- sleeve shirt, and sandals. Josh was similarly attired.

They walked across the expansive grass sports field, and into the village with its dirt road, and opened-fronted stores with their rusted corrugated roofs. The little restaurant, its low brick front surmounted by neat wooden shutters, was the neatest building in the village. Inside were eight round tables, each covered with a dark cloth. At each table were four padded chairs. Adorning the walls were prints of paintings depicting scenes of Singapore Island. Diffused lighting gave a warm glow to the russet interior. The owner, Jamal, was a short, heavy man, with thick black hair, and full lips that parted in a smile as Josh and Jerome entered.

He greeted them warmly, and showed them to a table.

"Good evening, gentlemen. You've had a busy day?"

"We have, Jamal," answered Josh, "and we've come to enjoy your curried prawns."

"That will be my pleasure. Anything to drink?"

"Not just yet, thank you," answered Josh. "How about you Jerome?"

"A glass of white wine with the dinner."

"Very good then. Two curried prawn dinners, and one white wine," said Jamal, and he turned, and walked to the kitchen.

A sheepish grin on his face, Josh looked at Jerome seated across the table. "It's about Anne."

Jerome looked intently at Josh. "I think you're in love." His face lit up with a smile.

"Jerome, I don't think I am; I know I am. I can't stop thinking about her. I've never felt this way about a woman. She's on my mind all the time. I have this wonderful feeling inside. It's like I'm on a high without using drugs."

"Josh, you've got a bad case of love." Jerome had a broad grin on his face.

"I may have a bad case, but I sure feel good," Josh grinned. "Now I know how you feel about Francine."

"I'm so pleased for you, Josh. Anne seems to be a really nice person. I just hope she feels the same way about you."

"I think she does. She seemed to enjoy our luncheon dates, and she was delighted with the way her parents welcomed me. I got along well with both of them."

"I said Anne's parents would love you. What you need Josh is a little more self-assurance. You have a lot going for you."

"Thanks, Jerome, but I don't have your talents, and a scholarship to Cambridge. I left school at sixteen, and began an apprenticeship with an engineering firm. Two years later I quit to join the Air Force and become an engine fitter. Five and a half years later I'm a junior technician." There was a tone of resentment in Josh's voice.

"I'd say that's quite an accomplishment for a guy whose mother died when he was eleven, and had to spend the next five years with an alcoholic father."

"You really think so?"

"Yes, I do, and lets not forget, you have the assurance of a job with the Singapore Harbour Police," replied Jerome emphatically. "Furthermore, I think Anne is the best thing that's happened to you."

"Well, I can't deny that. I'm just dealing with being in love for the first in my life. Before, I just used women. Now along comes a woman who really means something to me."

"I think it's great," Jerome smiled.

"Yeah, and it's all your fault, Jerome," said Josh grinning broadly. "The big question is, what are you going to do about this situation?"

"OK. First, I have to enquire about a 'purchase of discharge;' if it's possible, and reasonable. Having the assurance of a job should help considerably. But of course, before I do any of this, I have to ask Anne the big question."

"I guess that is important," said Jerome, and quite spontaneously, he enacted a proposal. "Dear Anne, I wish to tell you that I have these strange, but wonderful feelings when I am in your presence. This is so, because I believe I am in love with you. I earnestly hope that you share these feelings. If you do, please tell me. If not, I shall be the most dejected man in all Singapore, but in time I think I will overcome my deep disappointment. Dearest Anne, please tell me you love me, and you will make me the happiest of men." Jerome bowed as though acknowledging applause. "Do you think she could say 'no' to that?"

"Most probably not. But what makes you think I'm capable of such oratory? Furthermore, I think you're taking the mickey out of me," replied Josh with a broad grin.

Jerome was laughing. "Oh, but Josh, I hope Anne says 'yes.' I know how happy you would be."

"Jerome, this is almost too much for me. All of a sudden my life is being turned around. I've fallen in love for the first time ever, and I'm considering the possibility of marriage, and living and working in Singapore. That's a lot to think about."

"But Josh, it's so fantastic, so exciting. If Francine accepts my proposal, we'll have to wait three years, and then we'll go to another country. At most, you'll have to wait about one year. Start saving!"

Josh was looking intently at Jerome, his face wreathed in smiles. "You're a mover and a shaker, Jerome."

"No, just a maker of dreams."

Jerome and Francine strolled along Canning Road beside the park. An earlier rainfall gave freshness to the evening air. They had enjoyed the day together. In the afternoon they had seen It's a Wonderful Life, with Jimmy Stewart as the ambitious but despondent George Bailey, who is saved from committing suicide by Clarence, a bumbling angel, who then helps George save the small town of Bedford Falls from the greedy clutches of 'old man Potter.' The film had evoked laughter and tears. Now, as they passed a pathway leading into the park, Jerome stopped suddenly, and took hold of Francine's hands. He looked into her dark eyes, "Francine, I have to tell you I love you very much."

She smiled softly, "I know darling, and I love you too. I think you've been wanting to tell me this for some time."

"How did you know?" Jerome looked genuinely surprised.

"Oh, in so many ways, the look in your eyes, your attentiveness, your obvious delight at being with me." She continued to smile.

"It really shows that much?"

"Didn't you know darling, when you're in love it's written all over your face?"

"I guess it is." He smiled a little wistfully. "I have that wonderful excited feeling inside. I had it once before. That's how I knew I was in love again."

"It is a wonderful feeling," said Francine, and she pulled Jerome to her, and kissed his lips. This was the first time they had kissed, and letting go of Francine's hands, Jerome wrapped his arms around her, and held her close. He smelled the mild fragrance of her perfume, and the freshness of her thick black hair. He wanted to savour the moment. Suddenly, Francine pushed him away at arms length. She looked enquiringly at Jerome. "Tell me about that other time."

"Do I have to?"

"I want to know all about you my dear."

"It's a long story."

"I've got time." Francine was smiling at him.

"OK, but lets get a coffee, or better still, a glass of wine."

Jerome waved down a taxi, and asked for Raffles.

They sat in one of the lounges. Jerome ordered a wine, while Francine drank coffee, and ate an assortment of nuts. Then Jerome began his abbreviated narrative about Rebecca, and her discriminating mother. When he had finished, Francine shook her head slightly. "You really think her mother intercepted your letters?"

"I'm positive. Not only that, I'm sure she spun Rebecca a fantastic story about my having an affair with some exotic native woman."

"Mm, how romantic. Hot love in the tropics," Francine laughed.

"Francine, you surprise me."

"But my dear, I'm sure that does happen to some of these young men. They're miles from home, no significant restraints, and free to indulge their appetites. The temptations are considerable."

"You're so right. I see some of them. They're like children let loose in the sweet shop."

"But Jerome, tell me more about Rebecca's mother. Is she really as bad as you say?"

"When I said goodbye to your mother, following the lunch, she hugged me. I was so moved. Mrs. Millden never even shook my hand, not even when I said goodbye just before my departure for Singapore. ' I suppose Rebecca will keep us informed,' she said, and walked into her house. She was so cold. Your mother was so warm and loving."

"My mother's a very emotional person. She has an uncanny ability to judge character. But tell me, how do you feel about losing someone you were so in love with?"

"At first I was deeply hurt. I thought of involving my mother, but then I didn't think it fair to put my mother in the middle of what could become a tense situation. Mrs. Millden would have a way of belittling my mother, and I didn't want her to experience that. So I started seeing more of Singapore, and that's how I met you. One thing that is so reassuring for me is your mother's attitude. She's not judging me on the basis of where I live, or what my father does. She sees me for who I am. She truly appreciated my playing Beethoven. She wanted to hear more. The first time I played for Mrs. Millden, she could not bring herself to applaud. 'You play rather well,' she said. Your mother, on the other hand, was near ecstatic."

"She thinks highly of you, Jerome. After you left, she told me you are 'a good man.' And she's right."

About 11.20 in the evening, Julian Van Dyke parked his black Rover on Bras Basah Road a short distance from the Cathedral of the Good Shepherd. He and his wife, Lucia, Francine, and Jerome joined the annual pilgrimage to the Cathedral to attend Christmas Eve midnight Mass. Each year at this time, this service brought out the faithful and the not so faithful in a steady procession to the Cathedral. Before the four of them entered, they heard the choir's rendition of Joy to the World. As they entered the choir was beginning Away in a Manger. Already the Cathedral was full, but Julian saw a space for them only six rows from the front. Both he and Lucia were "up front" Catholics. By midnight, people were standing in the aisles. Soon a procession of altar boys appeared, followed by the Bishop and priests. One enthusiastic altar boy was swinging his thurifer through long oscillations, and very quickly the sweet aroma of incense permeated the air. Then the Mass began.

"In nominee Patris, et Filii . . ." intoned the Bishop. "Introibo ad altare Dei," he continued, and an altar boy responded, "Ad Deum qui laetificat . . . "

Jerome wondered if he would ever hear the Mass celebrated in English. But other thoughts filled his mind. Back home Christmas was seven hours away. His family would also attend midnight

Mass, and his mother would weep quietly for her absent son. For Jerome, this would be his final Christmas in Singapore. He wondered if he would ever return. He doubted it. An altar boy began reciting the Confiteor, and interrupted his musings. ". . . quia peccavi nimis cogitationes, verbo, et opere." Jerome reflected on the past week. Have I ("sinned exceedingly in thought, word, and deed")? He glanced at Francine. Dear Lord, always my thoughts of her are pure, and I have been thoughtful of my fellow humans. Then, as though to console him, the Bishop began "Aufer a nobis quaesumus, Domine iniquitates nostras." (Take away from us our iniquities). Suddenly, his thoughts turned to Josh. Dear Lord, let his love for Anne continue to grow, and may his plans to reside in Singapore with Anne as his wife work out. For a long time, Jerome had learned to offer spontaneous prayers rather than relying on prescribed ones."Deo gratias," said one of the altar boys. An appropriate response, thought Jerome, with a smile.

He realized the epistle had been read, as he heard the Bishop say "Munda cor meum ac labia mea." "Cleanse my heart and my lips . . . " The gospel was a short reading from the first chapter of Matthew. The sermon was predictable, and surprisingly short. Jesus, the Saviour of mankind, was born in a nondescript stable, with animals for company. Under such conditions was born the One who would change the course of world history.

The Mass continued, and the choir sang the Latin version of Adeste Fideles. A rich tenor was audible above the others in the choir. Jerome raised his eyes toward the altar. The Bishop was elevating the host, the body of Christ. Heads in the congregation bowed. Jerome thought the Bishop should be facing the people. Perhaps, one day. Shortly after, he rose, and followed Francine and her parents down the center aisle to the altar rails, where he knelt and received communion. He paused a moment, then rose and followed Francine back to his seat. Bowing his head, he said a prayer of thanksgiving for the many blessings he had received during his time in Singapore, then he looked up as the Bishop pronounced a final blessing, and said, "Ite Missa est." The choir began singing Silent Night, Holy Night, then, as one, the congregation joined in the singing of this quintessential Christmas carol. Not until the singing had finished, did the slow exodus from the Cathedral begin. Francine took Jerome's hand, "Merry Christmas, my darling," she said softly.

"Merry Christmas, dear Francine."

Outside, Lucia Van Dyke hugged Jerome. "A very happy Christmas my dear Jerome." He returned the greeting, and squeezed her husband's outstretched hand.

"Jerome," said Mr. Van Dyke, still holding Jerome's hand, "I'm so pleased you were able to be with us at Midnight Mass. It is so much a part of our Christmas celebrations."

"Thank you so much for inviting me, Mr. Van Dyke. In a few hours, my family will do the same."

"That's wonderful. I'm so pleased we did this for you."

With that, they strode after Francine and her mother, who were walking arm in arm along Bras Basah Road toward the car. Jerome was thinking how different this Christmas was from last year's. Before retiring for the night, Lucia Van Dyke wished Jerome a good night's sleep, and holding his hands, and looking at him with gentle eyes, said, "Jerome, my dear, you are a long way from home, and we want you to treat our home as yours." Then she squeezed his hands. "Good night, Jerome."

With tears in his eyes, he watched her walk away down the wide hallway. Entering his room, he sat in a chair, and reflected on all he had been blessed with this Christmas. He slept well this night.

For Jerome, this Christmas was unlike any he had celebrated. The Van Dyke's dinner table was comparable to that of the Millden's. The difference was the laughter and gaiety that filled the room. He was amazed at the amount and variety of food served, and the selection of wines. All this was beyond his parents' limited budget, yet he felt so at ease in the company of the eight people who sat at the table, and Lucia Van Dyke had much to do with this. Inevitably, Jerome was called upon to play, which he did, much to the delight of not only Mrs. Van Dyke, but also their guests, who marveled at Jerome's performance. The many requests almost exhausted Jerome's quite considerable musical repertoire, but he had to admit enjoying being the center of such attention, which did not go unnoticed by Francine, who whispered, "Tell me, darling, when do you give your next public performance?"

"I have to check with my agent," quipped Jerome. With that, he relinquished his seat at the piano, over the quiet protests of Francine's mother.

"Francine, I do believe you are responsible for this sudden stoppage in Jerome's playing."

"Oh mother, I just thought his hands needed a rest," and she smiled impishly at her mother.

The conversation flowed easily, and Jerome enjoyed socializing with the guests, among them a very bright young lawyer, building himself a lucrative practice within Singapore's business community. More than once that night, Jerome was told he should come to Singapore after he graduated from Cambridge. Lucia Van Dyke was hopeful, and Jerome found himself pondering his intention of going to America, though he knew the New World's social order would win out. He had lived too long in England.

"Darling, I hope you didn't stop because of me." Francine put her arm around Jerome's, and cuddled up to him.

"Why no, dear. I'm becoming conversant with the Van Dyke humour. But, I may yet give an encore."

"Now that would be wonderful. Shall I make an announcement?"

"Don't you dare," replied Jerome, a smile on his face.

"Now what are you two plotting?" asked Francine's mother.

"I was suggesting that Jerome give an encore," said Francine, smiling at Jerome.

"I think that's a wonderful suggestion."

"I've suddenly got a case of stage fright."

"My dear, I have the perfect remedy for that," replied Mrs. Van Dyke, and taking his arm, she led Jerome to the piano, to the delight of her guests. Then she whispered in his ear, "A little Beethoven, my dear."

Jerome smiled, and very soon the silence was broken only by the music of Beethoven sonatas, mixed in with some waltzes and ballades by Chopin. Jerome's playing put everyone in a restful mood, which provided a fitting conclusion to a delightful evening. Lucia Van Dyke just wished her future son-in-law would return to Singapore, rather than immigrate to America. As she had done on the previous evening, Lucia Van Dyke wished Jerome a good night's sleep, and thanked him for sharing his talent.

"It was my pleasure, Mrs. Van Dyke, and thank you again for your hospitality.

All of you have been so kind. This Christmas has been so memorable for me."

"You are welcome, my dear," and she hugged Jerome.

Once again, he found himself contemplating his great fortune at having met Francine.

Jerome had a week's leave, and the Van Dykes had invited him to stay with them. As business was slow, Francine decided this would be a good time to also take a few days off from work to spend with Jerome. Their time together was magical. They walked through Singapore's more attractive shopping areas, and stopped for coffee and pastries. They talked and laughed a lot. They were two young people very much in love, and at times, Jerome felt, that like Romeo, he also was in love with love. For both of them, this was a heady time, and yet each saw the beauty, and sincerity in the other. There were both strength and depth in their love. It was no passing fancy. Before Jerome's leave finished, he wrote home, and told his parents about his unforgettable Christmas. He had, of course, missed them, but the kindness of the Van Dykes had made Christmas truly memorable, and had helped ease the loneliness of being so far from home. While he told them about Midnight Mass and the excellent choir, he chose not to inform his parents about the lavish Christmas dinner accompanied by a wide selection of wines. "It was," he wrote, "a most enjoyable dinner." One day, he hoped he would be able to provide his parents with a similar fare.

⌇

Back in Changi, Josh and Jerome talked about their respective Christmas celebrations.

"This had to be my best Christmas ever," Josh told Jerome, "and for this I have to thank Anne and her family. Before dinner, we all held hands, while Anne's father said a grace. It was then I realized my Christmas lacked a spiritual content. Like you, Anne attended Midnight Mass with her family. Early in the afternoon, before most of the other guests arrived, I discussed with Anne, the possibility of becoming a Catholic. She was delighted that I was even considering it."

"With a name like Quinn you should make a fine Catholic," Jerome chuckled.

"It's Irish, isn't it?" said Josh thoughtfully.

"Begorrah it is. As Irish as Guiness and Patrick," replied Jerome in a pronounced Irish brogue. "The best Catholics are Irish."

"Christmas Day dinner was a gastronomic delight," Josh continued, oblivious of Jerome's jesting.

"Big word, Josh."

"I've been with you too long, Jerome," quipped Josh. " Seriously though, never have I seen so many different dishes on one table, nor such a selection of wines."

"Josh," interjected Jerome, "it was the same at Francine's. The table virtually groaned under the amount of food, and wine flowed like water. My mother would have been totally bewildered."

"And Jerome, the company was so congenial. Anne's sister and her husband were there, along with her mother's sister and her husband, her father's surviving brother, and two close family friends."

"One big, happy family," smiled Jerome.

"Yes, and the conversation never ebbed. Later in the evening, Anne and her sister entertained us. Her sister plays the violin. The only person missing was you, Jerome. You'd have made up a great trio. Doubtless, you were entertaining the Van Dykes' guests."

"I had to do something for a week's lodging," Jerome shrugged.

"That's right. I was forgetting, you spent a week at the Van Dykes'. You're a virtual son-in-law," smiled Josh.

"In potentia."

Josh showed a puzzled frown. Now you're confusing me with foreign terms."

"I'll explain later, old chap," smiled Jerome.

In the weeks following Christmas, Jerome, Francine, Josh and Anne were a virtually inseparable quartet. Josh enjoyed his second and third concerts. Again, Jerome was his mentor for each one. The four of them went to films, and talked and laughed over leisurely luncheons. Josh could not recall a time in his life when he had been so content. What saddened him was the thought that the quartet would soon cease to be. One evening he expressed his feelings to Jerome.

"You know, in two months I'll return to England, and you'll follow a month later. Hopefully, I'll return to marry Anne, and begin a new career here. But you'll remain in England for at least three years. I'm going to miss you, Jerome." Josh's voice was thick with emotion. "I've found such happiness here, and you've played such a part in it."

"I'm pleased to have done so, Josh, and I'm going to miss you, too. You've been a good friend. Sometimes I think I too, should return to Singapore."

"You should give it serious thought, Jerome. You mentioned people at the Christmas dinner suggesting you return to Singapore after completing your studies at Cambridge. With your education and brains you'd have all sorts of job opportunities here." There was conviction in Josh's voice.

Jerome was looking intently at Josh.

"But you know, I've always wanted to go to America. Maybe you and Anne should join Francine and me."

"No," replied Josh emphatically. "I like Singapore, and I think I'm going to enjoy being a mechanic with the Harbour Police. But I'll promise to write letters, as long as you reply."

"Letters from Singapore, by Josh Quinn. Sounds impressive."

"Probably not as impressive as Letters from America, by Jerome Callaghan," replied Josh, with a grin.

"Life is full of disappointments though, Josh. You make a good friend, and then that friend is out of your life. My mother will dread the day I leave for America. She loses a son and a daughter-in-law, and the Van Dykes lose a daughter and a son-in-law. ' The best-laid schemes o' mice an' men/ Gang aft agley.'"

"What's that about?"

"It's Robbie Burns reminding us that not all our best-laid plans work out."

"So often that's true," said Josh. "I just hope my ' best-laid scheme' works out."

"You know Josh? I think it will. Your request for discharge may yet come through. Just think, you might not even have to leave Singapore," and putting an arm around Josh's shoulders, added, "It's time for a coffee."

They went out to the NAAFI in the next building.

Jerome's remark to Josh about not having to leave Singapore proved prophetic. Two months prior to his departure date, Josh was called to the main administration office. There a sergeant informed him that the Base Commander wanted to see him. "I believe your purchase of discharge has come through," said the sergeant. Josh smiled. Then he was being ushered into the C.O.'s office. Group Captain Langlois was a rather short, hearty man. He greeted Josh warmly.

"Sit down Quinn. Now I rather think you'll be pleased to know your request for a purchase of discharge has been granted. Obviously, your grounds for this request were considered acceptable. I happen to know the Commissioner of Police. Fine chap. I phoned him when I read you had the assurance of a job with the Harbour Police. He spoke highly of you, and said the job would be a great opportunity for you. I must admit I liked the idea of one of our chaps joining the Singapore Police in that capacity. Now Quinn, show those fellows how well the Air Force trains our technicians. I understand your boss is also a former Air Force fitter?"

"Yes sir. He served twelve years, and was also discharged in Singapore."

"How interesting. You'll have a lot in common. Both fitters in the Air Force, and both have fallen in love with Singapore. It is a beautiful place. I also believe you have a lady friend here, Quinn. Indeed, the Commissioner's secretary."

"That's correct sir."

"Well Quinn, I must congratulate you on your taste in females. The Commissioner also told me the young lady plays for the Singapore Symphony."

"I must say sir, you know a lot about my lady friend," said Josh with a broad smile.

"Privilege of my position, Quinn, but I do wish you all the best in your future career in Singapore. I presume you have plans for a wedding in the near future?"

"Very definitely, sir. Now that my discharge will be in Singapore, Anne and I will probably marry later this year."

"Well that's wonderful. I like to see young fellows like you making a success of their lives. The chaps in the office will give you the details about your discharge. It will take effect early in June. Good luck, young man. All the very best in your new career, and in your marriage." Group Captain Langlois shook Josh's hand, and smiled warmly.

"Thank you sir," said Josh, smiling broadly. Then he saluted smartly, and left the C.O.'s office. The sergeant, who met him earlier, gave Josh a brief run down on the process. He would pay 500 Malay dollars to the chief accounting officer one month prior to his date of discharge. His uniforms he would leave at the main supply center on the base two days before his discharge. When Josh finally left the Admin. Office, he was practically floating on air. Wait 'til he saw Jerome. That evening he phoned Anne to tell her the good news. She cried.

"Oh Josh, darling, I'm so happy for you, and at the same time I'm happy for both of us. Now we can really make plans. I can't wait to tell my parents. They'll be so pleased. Can you come over this Saturday?"

"I certainly can," replied an equally excited Josh. "See you about eleven on Saturday."

"Can't wait."

"Goodbye Anne,"

"Goodbye my darling."

～

"So you don't have to return to England. Some guys get all the luck." Jerome was responding to Josh's good news.

"Just live right, Jerome," replied a smiling Josh.

"Josh, I'm so happy for you. It couldn't have happened to a nicer person. I just wish I was going to be here for your wedding."

"I wish you were too, because you were to be my best man."

"I guess one cannot do it by proxy?"

"No way. I'm wondering if my new boss may consider filling the role."

"On the other hand, you might consider the Commissioner, himself. After all, Commissioner's secretary marries former member of His Majesty's Royal Air Force."

"Sounds convincing, Jerome. Imagine, the Commissioner of Police as my best man."

"I'm jealous already."

"Well, eat your heart out," quipped a laughing Josh.

"Josh and Anne Quinn. I like it," said Jerome.

Geoff Dawson was delighted when Josh phoned, and told him the good news. He even suggested the possibility of Josh's starting earlier than September.

"Phone me later next week, and I'll have an answer for you, Josh."

"Thank you. I'll do that."

⌒

News of Josh's early discharge spread through the squadron like wild fire. Even Chief Bradley, usually so moody and cynical, congratulated him, and wished Josh the best in his new job.

"You're doing the right thing, Josh. This Air Force is no place for a young married man who has the opportunity of a good job."

Late in May the members of 205 Squadron gathered at Jamal's restaurant in Changi Village, to say farewell to Josh. Jamal put on an excellent smorgasbord, and Josh moved from table to table, and joked and reminisced with everyone in attendance. A few rose to make short, impromptu remarks about Josh.

"After some dalliances with ladies of dubious reputations, I am pleased to learn that Josh is now enamoured of a young lady of high repute. Indeed, if I may say, a woman, a wife, and a lady." The speaker was Eddie Burns. His last remark brought raucous laughter from everyone, and there were those who said he would still have made the remark had an officer been present. As was expected, Jerome spoke. He knew Josh would have been disappointed had he not.

"From the ladies of the night to a lady of the light, Josh has found a wonderful person with whom to spend his life. While Eddie is a little premature, Anne will become Josh's wife

sometime this year, and Eddie is right, she is every bit a lady."
Then raising his glass, he offered a toast. "I wish them both
happiness and good health throughout a long life together."
Everyone rose and joined in the toast. "To Josh and Anne."
Josh put a hand to his eyes, and began wiping away the
tears. Then, in a voice filled with emotion, he said, "I'm excited
about my immediate future, but I'm going to miss you fellows.
I'll miss Eddie's lectures, and Jock's advice, which I could never
quite interpret, and Geordie's sage comments." Laughter rippled
through the small restaurant. "Those of you who will be here
for my wedding are welcome to come. It will take place in the
chapel in The Good Shepherd Cathedral on the corner of Bras
Basah Road and Victoria Street. It will doubtless be the first time
in church for many of you, so come."

Josh talked much more than he drank, and when he finally
went and thanked Jamal for the excellent food, and the use of his
restaurant for the night, it was after 2a.m.

"You're very welcome, Josh, and I wish you much happiness.
You must bring your lady friend here for dinner soon."

"I will, Jamal. That's a promise. Anne will love your food."

"Thank you. I look forward to seeing the two of you soon."

Josh walked back to the barrack block with Jerome, Eddie,
Geordie, and Jock; it was a night he would long remember.

Three days before his discharge, Josh received a letter from a
nurse in England. Sheila Hanley, who worked at the County
Hospital in Northampton, had obtained Josh's address from
his father, a patient in the hospital, following a severe stroke.
She wrote to inform Josh of his father's condition. She had also
spoken with Harold Quinn's younger sister, who also wrote to
Josh. She knew the relationship between Josh and his father was
a contentious one. A three-week sea voyage would likely bring
Josh home to a deceased father. The aunt had informed Josh she
and her older sister would attend to all funeral arrangements.

Josh replied, informing his aunt of his situation, and his decision not to return to England. The aunt concurred fully in his decision, was pleased to learn about his job opportunity in Singapore, and congratulated him on his forthcoming marriage. "An Asian mix will be good for the Quinns," was her comment. Josh approved.

Josh regretted his relationship with his father. Fathers and sons were meant to be good friends, but this never happened to Josh. He experienced only the wrath of a bitter man. If ever he had a son, it would be different.

Ten days later, Josh received a telegram informing him of his father's death. While in hospital, the father never once asked about Josh.

⌒

Early in June, Jerome sailed for England, along with a few hundred other military personnel. Francine, Josh, and Anne were at the quay to wave farewell. A sudden blast of the ship's siren signaled the departure. Slowly, silently, the ship moved away, until the bow turned toward open water, and Jerome was lost from sight.

"There goes one of the best friends I've ever had," said Josh sadly.

"Maybe he'll be back," replied Anne, as she held Josh's arm.

"I don't think so, Anne. It's America for sure, and I just hope I'll be with him."

"Of course you will," replied Anne sternly. "Jerome's not going without you."

"Three years is such a long time," sighed Francine.

"You can trust Jerome," said Josh. "He's going to be studying for both of you."

"I know Josh. You're quite right, but three years still seems so long," and Francine dabbed her eyes with her handkerchief.

"Oh, Francine, we'll meet with you every week," enthused Anne, and letting go of Josh's arm, she hugged Francine.

"Thank you, Anne. I'll make it, because I know Jerome will."

It was Saturday, and just past lunchtime. They went into a small, attractive restaurant, and ordered appetizers with their wine.

Josh began work with the Harbour Police late in July. Geoff Dawson had successfully negotiated the earlier commencement date. At thirty-five, he was a young manager, and an excellent organizer. He worked well with people, and understood how to get the best out of his staff. He and Josh quickly formed a strong friendship. When Josh announced his marriage to take place in mid October, he asked Geoff Dawson to be his best man. Moved by the request, Geoff Dawson said he would be honoured to do so. Earlier, Francine had agreed to be Anne's maid-of-honour.

The day of the wedding was dull, and cloudy. The Squadron members who knew Josh, and were still in Changi, attended the wedding. Some fifteen showed up. This was an event they could not miss. Eddie Burns saw Josh as the prodigal son come home, only this homecoming was to the arms of the young lady soon to be his wife. Eddie sat in awed silence throughout the entire ceremony, which was short, simple, and quite beautiful. As a non-Catholic, Josh signed a pledge to raise their children Catholics. For Josh, who intended to convert, this was a mere formality. Excluded from the ceremony was a nuptial Mass, but the young priest who officiated spoke eloquently about marriage, and he impressed everyone present with his words.

"Anne and Josh," he began after their exchange of vows, "you have entered upon a special journey. This is both a spiritual as well as a physical journey that you will negotiate together. Each has to consider the needs of the other. Heed the advice of Saint Paul, and ' let not the sun go down on your wrath.' Talk about your differences, and do not be mute about them. Most importantly, pray together, and always seek answers through prayer. These tenets have guided my parents through thirty-six years of a beautiful marriage. Go now, Anne and Josh, and do the same. Before you do, I would like to pray a blessing over you, and placing a hand on each of their heads, he prayed the blessing God gave to Aaron:

> "The Lord bless you and keep you;
> The Lord make His face to shine upon you,
> And be gracious to you;
> The Lord lift up His countenance upon you,
> And give you peace."

Tears ran down Francine's cheeks. I would like that same blessing, when Jerome and I are married, she thought. Outside, as though the heavens had heard the blessing, the sun was shining, and a group of the Squadron members surged around Josh and Anne to congratulate them. Eddie Burns made a point of thanking the priest for "a truly memorable service. It was," he said, "simple and beautiful." Father Aloysius Gonzaga was most grateful.

Two days later, Francine sent Jerome a detailed account of the wedding.

End Part II.

Part III.

REALIZING A DREAM

THE TROOPSHIP steamed slowly along The Spithead, and then up the long channel into Southampton Harbour. Shortly before eleven o'clock on a sunny July morning, it docked. Already Jerome was missing the humid warmth, and colour of Singapore. For almost eighteen months he had savoured another country, and another culture. He had moved among different races, with their different traditions, and colourful dress, and engaging smiles. He had tasted and enjoyed a variety of exotic foods. For almost eighteen months he had not experienced a seasonal change, only humid heat, and warm rain. He had smelled the fragrance of frangipani and hibiscus. All this was so much more exotic than the drab environs of Eldon. There was within him a restlessness that he hoped his studies at Cambridge would curb, though only for a time. He had seen a world beyond England, and he wanted to see more. He was excited at the thought of seeing his family again after an absence of eighteen months, but he was also missing Francine. In the three weeks since leaving Singapore, he had written three letters to her. The third he would post from Southampton

Jerome decided to surprise his parents. Having completed the demobilization process the day after disembarking, he boarded a train for Eldon. The weather this early in July was warm enough for him to wear his Singapore clothes, though he did purchase a light pullover Shortly after one o'clock the train pulled into Eldon Station. He carried a stylish mock leather suitcase made in Singapore. The case opened out to accommodate a suit or trousers and shirts. One of Jerome's prized possessions, it was the product of a Singapore craftsman. In the case was a variety of gifts for the family members.

Jerome's father answered the single loud knock at the front door. He opened the door, and for a moment stood speechless, unbelieving.

"Jerome! It's Jerome!" and he threw his arms around his son, as the other family members came rushing to the door.

Soon his mother was embracing him, and crying, "Oh Jerome, you're home, you're home. You're back safely. Praise God." Tears flooded her eyes as she held her son. "You're darker, but still as thin as when you left."

"That's all the good food I ate."

Jessica came up to hug him, and he gave her a surprised look. She was very much a young woman. Jessica blushed a little as they hugged.

"It's so good to have you back. We've missed you."

"How are the studies?"

Before Jessica could answer, her mother interjected. "She's taking after you dear. She wrote her Higher School Cert exams in June. Next it's medical studies, we hope. But come inside. There are so many questions we have to ask, and so much to hear from you."

"Hello, big brother." It was Peter, still a little shy about hugging his brother.

"Hello Peter. You've grown. I can't call you little brother any more."

Now Peter was a gangly youth of fourteen.

Jerome put an arm around his brother's shoulder, and squeezed. Peter looked up, and smiled at Jerome. He was very proud of his elder brother.

Seated in the living room, Jerome responded to a litany of questions, while handing out a variety of gifts. Each one elicited an appreciative exclamation: for his mother, the delicate soup bowls with spoons that rested on the lids; the Omega wrist watch for his father; the ornate bracelet of Malayan silver for Jessica; and a genuine kukri for Peter. More than the gifts, more than the return voyage, more than Singapore, what Kathleen Callaghan was interested in was Francine Van Dyke.

"Tell me Jerome, is she really as lovely a person as you say she is?"

"Mum! I'm surprised you ask me that. Of course she is."

"Well dear, it's just that she seems so wonderful, and I'd hate for you to be deceived."

"She is a wonderful person, mum, as you'll find out one day."

"I'm sure I will, Jerome. I do trust your judgment."

"Thank you. I'm pleased to hear that." There was a touch of irony in Jerome's voice.

"Now Kathleen, let's not be critical, and too quick to form an opinion." James Callaghan did not want Jerome's homecoming marred by any unpleasantness.

"I'm sorry. I suppose I just want the best for our children." Kathleen Callaghan's tone was decidedly apologetic.

"And the best is what you will get dear, in education, and, I'm sure, in their choice of mates," replied her husband.

There was a sudden silence in the room, and Jerome's mother asked, "Tell me dear, whatever happened to Rebecca?"

Jerome sighed. Then looking at his mother he told her what he surmised had happened.

"That's a perfectly reasonable supposition. Certainly, Rebecca's mother would exploit any opportunity to end the relationship.But from what you tell me about Francine, I think this will be for the best. I'm a mother, my dear, and I worry about relationships."

Jerome smiled at her.

"I can see that, mum. Now, Francine and I have to get through the next three years."

"With your studies at Cambridge, those years will pass quickly," said his father. "Cambridge is your number one priority. It really is your future."

"You're right dad. Francine once said, 'No Cambridge, no Francine.'"

"Smart lady. She obviously realizes how important it is to your future." Then smiling at Jerome, he added, "I'm liking this Francine more and more."

It was late when Jerome finally went to bed. However, he did not retire before going up to his mother, putting his arms around her, and saying,

"I love you mum."

"I love you, too, my dear. I'm sorry if I sounded a little unkind toward Francine. I'm sure she is as lovely as you say. At least there's no interfering mother."

"Definitely not, and you're forgiven." Jerome was smiling.

He fell asleep thinking about Francine.

A few days later, Jerome was able to arrange a meeting with Alan. He was home for the weekend. Now that he worked in London, weekends at home were rare. He was enjoying the city's abundance of entertainment and exhibitions, but Jerome was a special friend, and Alan was looking forward to seeing him again. They met at Errol's, a cosy little coffee bar that was proving very popular and successful. Alan was already seated when Jerome walked in. He rose, and greeted Jerome warmly.

"Good to see you again old friend. I'm sure you've got lots to tell me."

"It's good to see you, Alan. I want to hear about your job in the big city."

"I thought you might want an update on Rebecca."

"Alan, that's water under the bridge, sad as it may be."

"Just one question, and I promise I'll say no more about the matter. May I assume you wrote to Rebecca?"

"Indeed you may. During the voyage out, I wrote her three letters. Then over the next two months, I wrote another seven."

"And no responses?"

"None. It was obvious to me what happened."

"Dear auntie. What a bitch."

"That's putting it mildly, Alan. By March, I gave up, and then I met Francine."

"And now Rebecca's engaged."

"Oh. Who's the lucky guy?"

"His name's Ronald Chisley. His father has a very successful plumbing and heating business, and Ronald is learning everything about it."

"Obviously, mother approves."

"Very much. He lives with his parents in their 2500 square-foot house, that has the latest in central heating, and boasts an impressive tiled entrance, and mostly hard wood flooring, and the three bathrooms have the latest in bathroom fixtures."

"All of which will impress Mrs. Millden. I can see why she approves of the young man. But I'm not going to contact Rebecca, especially now she's engaged."

"I think that's a wise decision, Jerome. But now tell me about Francine."

For the next two hours they talked, and drank coffee. Alan sat fascinated, as Jerome told him about Francine, Singapore, and his vacation retreat of Penang Island.

"And all I ever got to see was the east coast of England."

Jerome simply smiled. "But you seem happy with your life."

"Oh yes. I really can't complain. I enjoy being in London. It's a great city."

"No girl friend?"

"Nothing serious, although recently I've been dating a young lady who loves music. Already, we've been to three concerts together. Maybe you would like to join us for the next one. I think it's in two weeks time."

"Thanks Alan, but I think I'll leave you to enjoy it with your lady friend."

"Threesomes aren't your thing."

"No."

"When do you go to Cambridge?"

"Early in September."

"I always knew you would make it, Jerome, and I also know you'll graduate with honours."

"Well Alan, that's three years away. In the meantime there are things I have to do. Thanks for meeting with me. We'll do it again before I begin Cambridge."

"Always good to talk with you Jerome."

They shook hands, and went their separate ways.

University was stimulating and exciting. Jerome met interesting young men and women, some of whom, challenged his beliefs, while others enhanced them. He greatly enjoyed the world of higher mathematics. He loved the objectivity and the beauty of mathematics. Sadly, the study was not something he could discuss with his parents, but they derived satisfaction from his success in his studies, and from his being the first Callaghan to attend university. Next year Jessica would begin medical studies at Oxford. At seventeen she was too young, and so she was advised to take an additional year of sciences, which would include biochemistry. Meanwhile, Peter was moving inevitably toward university. James and Kathleen Callaghan had good reason to be proud of their children.

Time seemed to pass quickly at university. Immersed in his studies, Jerome had little time to dwell on his separation from Francine. He missed her, but their frequent correspondence brought them close to each other. Their letters proved a wonderful expression of their love, to which they added their respective brands of humour.

One day during a break late in the winter term, Jerome visited the cemetery where John Trethewey was buried. Inscribed on the headstone was, "His life and his gardens were things of beauty/ And he shared both with thousands." How very appropriate, Jerome thought. Buried beside John was Henrietta, his wife of thirty years. Sadly, they had no children. Jerome recalled John telling him, "You are the son I never had." We meet so few really beautiful people in our lives, Jerome thought, and you, John, were one such person in mine. Then Jerome spoke quietly,"You would have loved Francine, John, but I think you would have been disappointed that Rebecca was no longer in my life."

Jerome left the cemetery a little saddened.

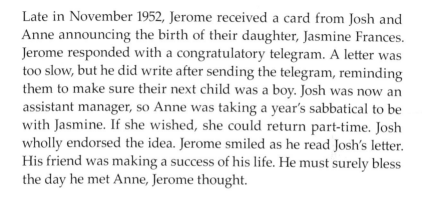

Late in November 1952, Jerome received a card from Josh and Anne announcing the birth of their daughter, Jasmine Frances. Jerome responded with a congratulatory telegram. A letter was too slow, but he did write after sending the telegram, reminding them to make sure their next child was a boy. Josh was now an assistant manager, so Anne was taking a year's sabbatical to be with Jasmine. If she wished, she could return part-time. Josh wholly endorsed the idea. Jerome smiled as he read Josh's letter. His friend was making a success of his life. He must surely bless the day he met Anne, Jerome thought.

The General Insurance Company of America, or The General, as it is affectionately called, is a highly innovative insurance company, and in the fifties was looking for energetic, educated young men to fill some key positions. The company was especially interested in persons with a background in actuarial science, and was having difficulty finding anyone with such a qualification. In a copy of the Seattle Times, Jerome read The General's ad. He answered, and within three weeks received a reply. The Company was interested in Jerome, and was prepared to send a representative to Cambridge to interview him. Jerome replied immediately, and was quickly informed that an Earl Menkov would be flying out to interview him. Jerome was excited at the prospect of having a job before he had even graduated.

On a dull afternoon in March 1953, Earl Menkov arrived in London. The next morning he took a train to Cambridge. There he interviewed Jerome. His intended one-hour interview extended to almost two. Clearly impressed with Jerome, Earl Menkov was convinced he had interviewed the man the company was looking for.

"Jerome, it's been a pleasure talking with you. You will be hearing from me very soon. In the meantime, I wish you success in your final exams."

"Thank you, sir. I appreciate your coming all the way to Cambridge to interview me."

"Jerome, I think I can say it's been worthwhile. Goodbye."

"Goodbye sir."

Earl Menkov left, and made his way to Professor Mallenby's office. He had arranged to take the professor out to lunch, and at the same time ask him pertinent questions about Jerome Callaghan.

Professor Mallenby, a lean man in his mid fifties, with an unruly shock of brown hair, had formed a high opinion of Jerome in the two years he had been his lecturer and tutor. He was hoping Jerome would choose an academic career, and benefit succeeding students with his considerable talent.

"So Mr. Menkov, were you suitably impressed with Jerome Callaghan?"

Professor Mallenby was noted for his directness. The two men were seated in one of Cambridge's small, intimate restaurants. The professor thought Earl Menkov would approve of the menu, and he was not mistaken.

"I was most impressed, not only with his academic achievements, but also with Jerome, personally. He seems to be a young man of integrity."

"Well then, Mr. Menkov, we need say no more, but, I should add, the academic world is going to lose a young scholar to business."

"That may be true, professor, but you know, Jerome will still be able to pursue his interest in mathematics, and at the same time have a rewarding career."

Professor Mallenby smiled. "Just don't take all our bright young graduates."

"Just the best," said Earl Menkov with a chuckle.

"Thank you for lunch, Mr. Menkov. You must come back sometime, and visit our historic town."

"You know, professor, I would like to do that. Goodbye. Thank you very much for your time."

"My pleasure, Mr. Menkov. My pleasure."

Professor Mallenby could not help but think that Jerome Callaghan would go all the way to the top of The General. He wont be satisfied with anything less, he thought.

Earl Menkov walked out of the restaurant into the fading sunlight. He was certain the company president would endorse his choice of Jerome Callaghan.

Jerome graduated with first-class honours. The Convocation was in late May, and attending this ceremony were, not only his parents, and Jessica and Peter, but also the Van Dykes. Jerome was thrilled that they had made a point of arriving in time for his convocation.

If "parting is such sweet sorrow," then reuniting is much sweet ecstasy.

Certainly, this was true of the reunion between Jerome and Francine, at Heathrow Airport. They literally ran into each other's arms, and laughed and cried for joy. It brought tears to her mother's eyes, and a broad smile to her father's face.

"Oh my darling," sobbed Francine, "it's so good to see you. Three years is too long to be apart."

"I've thought about this moment every day for three years," replied an excited Jerome. Then he turned to greet Francine's parents.

First Mrs. Van Dyke, and then her husband embraced Jerome, and spoke their joy at seeing him again.

"My dear Jerome," said Mrs. Van Dyke, "you haven't changed; Still the same tall, handsome young man, and congratulations on your final results. First class honours. Marvellous."

"Yes Jerome, congratulations," echoed her husband. "Outstanding results."

Francine put her hands against Jerome's head. "Mmm. Still the same size," she laughed.

"Oh, Francine, you're very naughty," said her mother, with a smile.

"Thank you for being here for my convocation. I really appreciate your doing this."

"Jerome, my dear," said Francine excitedly, "you don't think we would miss your convocation. We've waited three long years for this event."

"Oh Francine, you're so wonderful," said Jerome with a grin.

"Now, we take a train from here to Eldon, and then we'll take a taxi to your Hotel. I was going to suggest going over to the house to meet the rest of the family, but I think you'll want to sleep after such a long flight."

"I think so too, Jerome," said Mrs.Van Dyke. "Lets keep the visiting until tomorrow."

"Good idea. Phone us tomorrow, when you're ready."

"Jerome. If you don't mind, I'd like to come with you, and meet your family. Just let me freshen up a little," said Francine.

"You're sure you wont fall asleep?" said Jerome with a silly grin.

Francine's look was ample reply.

Kathleen Callaghan was nervous about the Van Dykes' visiting her home. Jerome had shown her photographs of their home, and the beautiful garden. He assured his mother that Mr. and Mrs. Van Dyke were coming to see his parents, not their house, nor the garden that would never be. Jerome's mother had added a flower box to the downstairs windowsill, and presently it was full of petunias. Even the small back yard now boasted a large wooden half-tub overflowing with petunias, delphiniums, peonies, and liatris.

"You know," said Jerome, "Mrs. Van Dyke will be impressed."

"You're just saying that to make me feel better," replied his mother with a smile. But Jerome was not wrong.

The taxi pulled up outside the Callaghan's house on Salisbury Street. The driver wished Jerome and Francine a cheery "goodnight." Julian Van Dyke had tipped him generously. Jerome ushered Francine inside, where his mother and Jessica waited excitedly.

"Mum, meet Francine." Jerome had an arm around her waist.

Mrs. Callaghan held Francine's hands, and looked at her with soft, blue eyes.

"Welcome, Francine. I've been so looking forward to meeting you. Jerome has, also, with great impatience." She smiled. "Francine, my dear, you really are as lovely as your photographs," and she embraced Francine.

A little embarrassed, Francine returned the embrace.

"Thank you, Mrs. Callaghan. I've also been looking forward to meeting you. Jerome has told me much about you."

"A biased view, of course." Mrs. Callaghan laughed softly, as she turned to Jessica.

"Francine, I'd like you to meet my daughter, Jessica."

"Oh, Jessica, my maid-of-honour. So good to meet you," and they embraced each other warmly. "We have some discussing to do." She held Jessica at arms length. "I must say, I have a most attractive maid-of-honour."

"Runs in the family," chuckled Jerome.

Just then Peter entered the room. His mother took his arm, and introduced him to Francine.

"Francine, this is Peter, my youngest. Jerome used to call him, 'little brother,' but as you can see, that's hardly appropriate." Peter smiled shyly.

"Hello Peter." Francine held out her hand, and Peter shook it gently.

"Hello Francine." He couldn't take his eyes off her. At seventeen, Peter was becoming very conscious of female beauty.

"Come and sit down, my dear." Mrs. Callaghan directed Francine to a comfortable easy chair. "You must be tired after such a long flight."

"I am. Which is why I wont stay long. I hope you don't mind, Mrs. Callaghan."

"My dear Francine, I'm surprised Jerome brought you over this evening."

"The truth is," replied Francine, "I couldn't wait to meet you."

"Oh, that's sweet of you, dear, and I'm most flattered, but you must rest. First, let me make you some tea," and Mrs. Callaghan disappeared into the kitchen.

"So Francine," began Jessica, "I have to get your approval about what to wear."

"Oh, Jessica, I'm sure you're like Jerome, and have impeccable taste." Francine smiled at Jerome.

"Jerome likes to think he's the family's sartorial advisor," Peter interjected quietly.

"Well said, Peter," Jessica smirked.

"Oh dear," said Francine, "have I touched a sore point?"

"Not really. It's just that my dear brother sees himself as something of an authority about dress. Right Jerome?" said Jessica.

Just then, Mrs. Callaghan returned with tea and assorted biscuits.

"Pay no heed to Jerome, my dear. I'm sure you'll love what Jessica has chosen."

"Mother!" said Jerome, "You were eavesdropping."

"No dear. Just being an attentive mother. Now Francine, how do you like in your tea?"

"Straight, with a little honey. Thank you."

"You know," continued Mrs. Callaghan, "I want to say how good it is that you and your parents, are here for Jerome's convocation."

"Oh, we weren't going to miss that, Mrs. Callaghan. It's almost as important as the wedding." Francine smiled at Jerome, who had a quick reply.

"Almost! My dear, that's an understatement."

"Jerome, how could you?" said his mother. "I'm surprised at you. Your wedding is the most important day of your life." She looked at him sternly, tea pot in hand.

"Well said, mother. Put Jerome right," quipped Jessica.

Jerome looked at Francine, and began to blush. He knew he had said the wrong thing.

"Now children, this is no way to behave in front of Francine."

"Oh, Mrs. Callaghan, you're forgetting, I had almost fourteen months of Jerome's humour."

"You poor thing," said Jessica quietly. Then, before Jerome could say anything, she added, "By the way, Francine, we'll be having a rehearsal on Saturday morning, at ten o'clock."

"Why don't we meet for breakfast in the morning, at the hotel?" suggested Francine. "I believe the food is very good."

"What a wonderful suggestion. We never eat breakfast out," said Mrs. Callaghan.

"Jessica can fill you in about the rehearsal," said Jerome. "So what time?"

"Shall we say ten o'clock?"

"That will be fine, Francine," replied Mrs. Callaghan. "We'll see you tomorrow at the hotel."

"I'll phone for a taxi," said Jessica, and went into the hall.

Jerome accompanied Francine to the hotel. Before getting out, she kissed him.

"It's wonderful knowing I'll see you tomorrow," said Jerome. "I'm looking forward to breakfast."

"So am I darling. See you in the morning." Francine closed the door, and walked up the short flight of steps into the hotel.

"Back home, gov'nor?" said the driver.

"Right," answered Jerome, and the cab sped away to Salisbury Street.

When Jerome entered the house, his mother was waiting for him.

"Oh Jerome, my dear, Francine is so beautiful. She reminds me of a film star. Such lustrous hair, and clear dark skin, and she seems to have a personality to match her beauty."

"You're so right, mother. She really does, and I consider myself a fortunate man."

"I hope you'll be happy together."

"I'm sure we will. Now I'm going to bed. It's been an exciting day."

"Just one piece before you do."

"OK." and he sat at the piano, and played Jesu, Joy of Man's Desiring, and Kathleen Callaghan sat and reminisced, and cried silently for the son she was soon to lose.

Shortly after nine-thirty, a taxi drove the Callaghans to the Swan Hotel that overlooked the Tarnley River. Francine was in the lobby with her mother. Jerome was the first to enter, closely followed by his mother. Lucia Van Dyke rose, and moved toward Jerome's mother.

"Mrs. Van Dyke, at last we meet, and what a pleasure." Kathleen Callaghan held out a hand, which Lucia Van Dyke enclosed in both of hers.

"Oh please, it's Lucia, and you are Kathleen, a lovely name. I'm so pleased to meet you," and she embraced Kathleen. "So at last, I meet Jerome's mother. You know, I have sat and listened to your son play so beautifully, and I have longed to meet the parents of this talented young man, and finally I do. You are James, his father." She shook James' hand, and smiled. James Callaghan returned the greeting warmly. "Now I would like you to meet my husband, Julian." He had just entered the lobby, and was walking toward the group.

"Good morning Mr. and Mrs. Callaghan." He shook their hands warmly, and began directing them toward the dining room.

"Father, called Francine, "say hello to Jessica and Peter."

"Oh, my apologies. I really am pleased to meet you, Jessica and Peter. You're tall like your brother."

"Yes," said Peter, shyly. "But not quite as tall."

Then looking at Jessica, Mr. Van Dyke said quietly, "and you young lady, have your mother's good looks." He smiled, and Jessica blushed.

The food was good, and the conversation flowed. Seated next to Francine, Jessica was able to give her the details about Saturday's rehearsal.

"You'll like Father Jardine. He's young, and charismatic, so he's not stuck in the old ways. Jerome mentioned you would like an Old Testament blessing to close the ceremony. I'm sure Father Jardine will approve that."

"I'm sure he will," said Jerome. "He has a musical background, and has introduced new hymns. He's even talked about a Mass in English, much to the concern of the traditionalists, but that requires Vatican approval. I find him refreshing."

"I'm so pleased to hear that," said Francine. "Actually, our choice of music is quite traditional, though Jerome wants Jesu, Joy of Man's Desiring played on the organ. It's for his mother."

"Oh, she'll love that," said Jessica.

My friend, Marlene, has offered to sing at the wedding. She has a beautiful soprano voice, and has already sung at The Royal Opera House, Covent Garden."

"You said 'yes,' of course." Francine was smiling at Jessica.

"I'm going to," replied Jessica.

Jerome's father was busy questioning Mr. Van Dyke about his business, and Singapore, while the two mothers discussed the joy of seeing their children grow up and succeed, and the sadness at seeing them leave home for more distant places.

"I lose a son and a beautiful daughter-in-law, and you, Lucia, lose a daughter and a son-in-law." There were tears in Kathleen Callaghan's eyes.

"Oh, my dear, you're so right, but we can't hold onto them forever. We have to let them make their own way in life, and hope their decisions will be good ones. I look at Jerome, my dear, and I believe he has made wise decisions. I believe he's going to be very successful." Lucia looked at Kathleen with her soft, dark eyes.

"I wont argue with that, Lucia. He's known for years that he'd go to America. The job opportunity, of course, is most recent. But, yes, I think he'll be successful. He'll make a good life for himself and Francine in America."

The tears had gone. Talking about their children was good therapy. Both mothers realized what a blessing their children were.

"Well Kathleen, have you finished analyzing the children's behaviour?" Her husband was smiling at her.

Before she could reply, Lucia responded. "We have James, and we have concluded there's no need for concern."

"I'm pleased to hear that," replied James Callaghan. "In fact, I could have told you that," he chuckled.

"Oh, but we mothers worry more than you men," replied Lucia Van Dyke with a smile.

As befitted the occasion, the Convocation was formal and dignified. Jerome looked handsome in his tasseled mortarboard, and blue-fringed gown. An admiring mother looked at him through tearful eyes, and smiled. This, she thought, is the first part of his dream accomplished. Francine was seated between her mother and Jerome's. Outside, May was a profusion of blossoms, and the sunlight danced and sparkled on the nearby Cam River, and filtered through the stained glass windows of the great hall. With the entry of the professors and graduates, a choir sang Let All the World in Every Corner Sing. The President of the University Senate addressed the class of 1953, then one of the deans called the roll of graduates. One by one they walked to the stage to receive their diplomas. Then it came, the announcement Jerome's parents and Francine so eagerly awaited. Jerome Patrick Callaghan was graduating with the highest honours in mathematics. The entire audience rose and applauded, as Jerome walked slowly to the stage to receive his diploma. He chose to relish the moment. The President congratulated him, and Jerome bowed his head, and smiled. His mother wept tears of joy as she embraced an ecstatic Francine. For James Callaghan, this was a very proud moment. Immediately behind them, Alan whispered, "I knew it. Nine years ago I knew he would be the best."

After the ceremony, Jerome received a steady stream of congratulations, including an especially warm greeting from Professor Mallenby.

"You have a very talented son," he told Jerome's parents. "Sometimes I thought he did not realize how talented he is. I wish Jerome every success with the insurance company. I fully expect him to be president one day." Then looking at Jerome, he added, "Now Jerome, stay in touch. I want to hear how you're making out on the wrong side of the Atlantic."

He smiled at Jerome, and shook his hand. "A pleasure meeting you Mr. and Mrs. Callaghan, and smiling at Francine, he said," A pleasure meeting you Miss Van Dyke, and congratulations on your forthcoming marriage."

"Thank you, Professor Mallenby."

"Then you're off to America."

"Yes Professor."

"You're both very adventurous, and I wish you success."

"Thank you," replied Francine. "I'm really excited, and I have such confidence in Jerome."

"Well you might, my dear. Well you might," said Professor Mallenby.

Then he was off, his tousled hair, and red-fringed gown blowing in the spring breeze.

The dinner was delicious. Julian had chosen a restaurant noted for its excellent cuisine, and overlooking the Cam River. It was an excited, garrulous group that entered The Maitre Chef Restaurant shortly after four that memorable May afternoon. Julian had also arranged the seating so as to mix the families. Jerome's mother sat beside Lucia. Across from them sat their respective spousal in-laws. To Lucia's left sat Jerome, and beside him was Francine. Across the table from them were Jessica, Alan, and Peter, who sat next to his mother. Jerome's father conversed at length with Francine. He was particularly interested in her visit to America, and talked about Jerome's childhood desire to immigrate there.

"And now it's a reality," said Francine.

"Yes, indeed, and I envy him."

Beside him, Julian was engrossed in conversation with Jessica, and Peter had the opportunity to find out how Alan was enjoying London.

Dinner began with a zucchini soup with herbs, followed by chicken with lemon sauce, and artichokes in a parmesan- cheese sauce. The salad was pear-ginger Waldorf. Dessert was an open-face peach pie, followed by tea, coffee, and liqueurs. So delighted was Julian with the dinner, he requested the presence of the chef to congratulate him. A rather embarrassed man in his forties appeared, and was greeted with "A toast to the chef," chanted in unison with a clink of glasses.

"Thank you ladies and gentlemen. This is a first," replied a slightly bewildered chef.

"You deserve it chef, and we thank you," said Julian.

"And I believe congratulations are in order for Jerome."

"Thank you, chef," replied Jerome.

The chef smiled, and quickly returned to his kitchen.

The train for London left at seven, which allowed time to connect with the ten o'clock train for Eldon. Two tired families stepped off the train in Eldon, and took taxis to their respective dwellings. A week later, Jerome and Francine were married at Saint Paul's Catholic church in Eldon.

Like that of Josh and Anne, Jerome and Francine's wedding was small and beautiful, and included a Nuptial Mass. Jerome chose a blue ruffled shirt to go with his gray dress suit. Alan was similarly attired. Francine wore a simple, ankle-length white dress, with long sleeves, and a pillbox style hat with a veil. Jessica wore a similar style dress in a soft shade of yellow, and matching shoes and gloves. Francine's father smiled proudly as he walked her down the aisle. Lucia and Kathleen sat in a pew near the front, and cried quietly. In the choir loft, Marlene sang the moving Laudate Dominum. By the end, even Alan had tears in his eyes. During the exchange of vows, Jerome and Francine looked into each other's eyes, and smiled, as each in turn said, "I do." The church was filled with parishioners who had known Jerome since his childhood. They were, of course, curious to see a bride from Singapore. For most of them, that was a distant, unknown country, and they were surprised to hear Francine speak fluent English. Near the end of the Mass, Marlene sang The Our Father in English. When she finished, Father Jardine placed a hand on each of Jerome and Francine's heads, and prayed the blessing requested by Francine:

> "The Lord bless you and keep you;
> The Lord make His face to shine upon you,
> And be gracious to you.
> The Lord lift up His countenance to you,
> And give you peace."

Francine and Jerome looked at each other with tearful eyes. Francine mimed "I love you," and Jerome nodded. Then they rose, faced the congregation, and began their slow walk down the aisle to the music of Mendelssohn's Wedding March. As they emerged from the church, the sun shone warmly from a cloudy sky, and a crowd of well-wishers besieged them. Young women looked enviously at Francine, and congratulated her. "She is so beautiful," she heard a teenage girl say softly to a friend. Another said, "I hope they'll always be this happy." Why not? Francine thought. We've waited long enough. What both of them were thinking was that in two days they would be saying goodbye, and beginning a long journey to another country, and a new life. Excitement mingled with sadness.

No one likes goodbyes, especially when they signal a long, and a distant separation. James and Kathleen dreaded the departure of Jerome and Francine, as much as did Julian and

Lucia Van Dyke. Jerome's mother did not linger over this farewell. She looked at Jerome and Francine,

"This isn't easy, but I told myself I wasn't going to cry. God bless you both. I'll pray for you every day."

Then she hugged each of them in turn, as did Jerome's father, who reminded them to never stop loving each other.

"All the days of our lives, dad. All the days of our lives," replied Jerome.

Then with Francine he walked out to a waiting taxi. Inside, Kathleen and James said their goodbyes to Lucia and Julian, who then joined Jerome and Francine in the taxi.

Kathleen Callaghan walked outside, and watched the taxi turn off Salisbury Street toward the Eldon Station. Then she went inside and cried.

At Heathrow Airport, farewells were repeated.

"I'm not going to cry," said Lucia, as she held her daughter. "I know you have a wonderful future ahead of you, and you'll have a wonderful life together. God bless you, my dear Francine."

Then she turned to Jerome.

"Look after each other, and never go to bed angry." She laughed softly, as she put her arms around Jerome.

"I told dad we'll love each other all the days of our lives.".

"Do that, my dear, and God bless you. Write as soon as you get to America."

She hugged Jerome, and walked away slowly.

Julian hugged his daughter, and they expressed their mutual love, then taking hold of Jerome's hand, he said,

"Take good care of each other, and stay in touch."

He gave Jerome a quick hug, and joined Lucia. They watched Jerome and Francine disappear down the long hallway to the flight check in entrance. Julian looked at Lucia, and said softly,

"Well, my dear, now there are just the two of us."

Lucia Van Dyke snuggled up to her husband.

⌒

The 747 climbed steeply into a cloudless sky. Jerome placed his hand on Francine's, and smiled at her. The last time I left England, he thought, was on a slow boat to Singapore. This time I'm on a fast plane to America. Francine closed her eyes, and began to sleep. All these farewells were too exhausting.

End Part III.

Part IV

FOR PARENTS TO MARVEL

T HREE YEARS had passed since Jerome and Francine left England, and they had accomplished much in that time. The drive to Lakeshore Boulevard took over an hour. When they drove into the wide semicircular driveway, Francine was standing at the large, ornate doorway. Jerome stopped the car under the tall portico. Francine stepped out, opened the door for Jerome's mother, and greeted her enthusiastically.

"Oh mum, it's so good to see you."

The two embraced each other warmly.

"And it's good to see you, my dear. Now where's my little granddaughter?"

"She's inside, sleeping. Hello dad. You're looking well."

James Callaghan walked up to his daughter-in-law, and hugged her.

"And you're looking as beautiful as ever."

Then he stopped, and looked around.

"I didn't think you'd have a palace already. You'll have to give us a guided tour later on."

Jerome's mother stepped into the spacious hallway, and gasped.

"Oh my goodness. You could fit our house in the hallway. James darling, isn't it beautiful?"

"It is. I was just saying to Francine, I didn't think they'd have a palace so soon."

"Now let me show you your bedroom," said Jerome.

His parents were in for more surprises. Their bedroom had an en suite bathroom, a feature they were unfamiliar with. This was luxury, and they relished it.

Having rested and showered, Jerome's parents came down for dinner, and Kathleen held her first grandchild. She cooed and whispered to baby Frances, held the tiny, curled fingers, and marveled at her delicate beauty.

"Oh James, look at her. Isn't she adorable?"

"She is indeed," replied James. "She has her parents' hair, and her mother's eyes."

The evening was warm, so they ate dinner on the patio.

"Jerome darling, this house must have cost you a fortune" said his mother.

"Not really," replied Jerome. "It was a quick sale. The previous owners were experiencing financial problems, and they were happy to accept our offer."

"One person's misfortune, you're good fortune," said Jerome's father.

"Something like that."

"Our bedroom is so large," added his mother. "It's going to take some getting use to."

"Just enjoy it mum."

"Oh. I will."

Both James and Kathleen were beginning to experience jet lag, and they retired shortly after dinner.

❦

"Admiring the view, dad?"

Jerome's father was up early, and decided to walk around the extensive property. He was in the back, looking toward the orchard.

"It's beautiful, Jerome. You picked a wonderful place to live. The water is so restful."

"It is. We were looking for waterfront property, and were fortunate to find this."

"So much land," said Jerome's father, looking around." You could put our house in here four times, and still have a garden. You've done well, son."

Jerome placed his arm around his father's shoulder.

"Thanks dad for always encouraging me."

"You know, Jerome, I couldn't see all your talent go to waste. It's been great seeing you break away from those social restraints. The first Callaghan to do so, and you know son, your sister and brother will do the same. I get excited just thinking about it."

He smiled at Jerome, who squeezed his father's shoulder. Together they walked down to the lakeshore. From the verandah off the living room, Francine watched this display of filial affection. Inside the spacious house, Kathleen Callaghan caressed her infant granddaughter, and gazed fondly at her. She knew Frances' parents had ambitious plans for their daughter. She was, after all, a privileged child, but she would not be spoiled. Just then, Francine entered.

"Mum, if you put Frances in her carrycot, I'll show you our property."

"Now that, I would like. I'm dying to look around your parkland." Kathleen smiled at Francine.

"Mum, it's not quite that big."

"But it's big," and she gently placed her grandchild in the carrycot, and followed Francine through the front door, into the front garden. The house was situated sixty feet from the road, allowing for a wide, semicircular driveway. The area inside the driveway was covered with juniper, and low flowering bushes. Linking arms with her mother-in-law, Francine walked slowly, stopping to identify flowers and bushes, and talk about how she and Jerome had searched long and carefully for a house that appealed to both of them, and had waterfront.

"I wanted a garden that reminded me of the one in Singapore, and Jerome wanted a house that was spacious, and full of light," Francine told Kathleen. "Finally, in October of fifty-four we found this one, and fell in love with it, and bought it. Jerome's recent promotion has helped with the financing."

Jerome's mother stopped, and looked at the portico.

"It really is beautiful. It's everything Jerome dreamed of as a boy," she said softly. "At fifteen, he knew America was where he'd realize his dream," and looking at Francine, she added, "and to share it with someone like you, my dear, is more than he dreamed of."

"Oh mum, how sweet of you to say that. I think we're blessed to have each other."

"You're so right, Francine. Cherish the relationship."

"Come, let me show you around the back," said Francine, smiling.

Kathleen Callaghan felt such a love for her daughter-in-law. Jerome had chosen well. The two of them continued around to the back. There a large patio stretched the width of the house, and extended out some fifteen feet. It comprised large, irregular shaped stones of different colours, set in cement. In the center was a large, circular cedar table that could seat twelve people. Jerome believed a round table was more conducive to good conversation. Flowers, and flowering bushes occupied much of the garden. Situated some twenty feet from the patio were two large, round flowerbeds. Each was seven feet in diameter, and thirty feet apart, with another fifteen feet on either side. They were Francine's special flowerbeds, one for each mother. Her selection of flowers ensured colour and blossoms from early spring to late fall. Pointing to the flowerbeds, Francine said,

"These are dedicated to the two mothers in my life. The one on the right, to you, mum; the other one to my mother."

"What a beautiful gesture, my dear."

Kathleen looked at the colourful herbaceous border, and the tall, wide petaled hibiscus in the center.

"Thank you so much Francine."

"You're most welcome mum. It's my way of keeping you near."

Francine felt her mother-in-law squeeze her arm, and draw her close. They walked on through the orchard to the small dock, and joined Jerome and his father on the twenty-seven foot Bayfield sail boat.

"Next to me and Frances, this is Jerome's greatest love," said Francine laughing.

"Oh my goodness," uttered Jerome's mother. "Two cars and a boat, and all this property. It's too much for me," she laughed.

"On Friday we'll sail up to Bothell. We'll have lunch at an excellent lakeside restaurant, and then sail back." said Jerome.

"Sounds wonderful," said his mother. "I'm going to miss this luxury when I get home."

"You can always stay," said Jerome.

"Thank you my dear, but I don't think that would work."

"It's tempting," replied her husband, "but I think you're mother's right." He smiled wistfully at his son.

"It's time for lunch," Francine interjected. "I've a delicious chicken cacciatore," and she led the way off the boat, closely followed by Jerome's mother holding the carrycot.

The cacciatore was delicious, as was the lunch on the Friday at the Lakeside Bistro. There, Jerome introduced his parents to Mario, the owner. Consistent with his Greek heritage, Mario greeted them effusively. Kathleen Callaghan was a little overwhelmed.

"Mario's convinced there's Greek in my background."

"Absolutely. The English don't have black hair like Jerome's." He smiled at Jerome's mother. "I think there has to be a little Greek on your mother's side. Just look at her beautiful black hair."

"Mario flirts with all the ladies," said Francine, smiling.

"But how is my littlest lady?" and Mario looked into the carrycot at Frances, who smiled at him.

"Oh, she is beautiful like her mother."

"You see what I mean, mum. Never misses a chance to flirt," said Francine.

"Now ladies, may I get you something to drink before you order?" Mario flashed a dazzling smile at Francine and Kathleen.

Jerome's mother enjoyed the food. For the first time in her life she tasted lobster in a succulent sauce, and accepted Mario's choice of a Riesling wine. James chose the beef stroganoff, along with Mario's choice of Merlot. This was one way in which Jerome's parents could share in his success. Over lunch he told them about a trip they would take to the Mount Baker area.

"You said you wanted to see the mountains, and if possible walk on snow. Mount Baker is the place."

"You'll love it, mum," said Francine, "especially if the weather stays sunny."

Before lunch was over, Mario placed a slice of strawberry cheesecake in front of Jerome's mother and father.

"With my compliments, for each of you to enjoy. Enjoy your vacation, and come again before you leave."

"Why thank you Mario," said a surprised James Callaghan.

Mario patted Jerome's shoulder as he passed.

"Thank you, Mario. See you again, soon."

The winter of '55/'56 was particularly cold, and the snow was deep on Mount Baker. Even in July there was snow close to the lodge. Alongside the long, winding road to the lodge, the trees and bushes were lush green. Jerome's parents were fascinated. Neither had seen so much snow, nor had they been at such an altitude before. The snow, softening under the July sun, was easy to walk on, and easy to compress into snowballs, which Jerome's mother did. She could not resist the temptation to throw one at Jerome. With unerring accuracy, she struck her target.

"Mum!" A surprised son turned to see his mother laughing, and applauding herself. Jerome's response was quick, but his aim was poor. Before he could repeat, a second snowball found its mark Snow splattered over his head. Francine was encouraging Jerome's mother, who adroitly avoided a missile from Jerome.

"Jerome, you should surrender to a superior force, before being further humiliated," chuckled Francine.

"Fancy being out thrown and out hit by your mother," Jerome grinned. "Mum, where did you learn to throw like that?"

"My brothers showed me how to skip stones on the lake near our home. I became good at it, and at knocking tin cans off fences."

"You never told me you were a tomboy, mum."

"She was until I came along." James Callaghan had been watching, greatly amused by his wife's throwing ability.

"That's when I had to start behaving like a lady," replied Kathleen with a wide smile.

In the little village of Glacier, where the mountain road begins, Jerome parked outside a quaint little restaurant noted for its excellent chicken-in-a-basket. James was impressed with the friendliness of the waitress, a jovial, rather rotund lady.

"Now you folks aren't from around here." Her voice was loud but friendly.

"No, indeed not," replied Kathleen. "My son and his wife and baby live in Seattle. My husband and I are from England. We live in a small town just west of London."

"Now there's one place I'd sure love to go."

"London?" said Kathleen.

"Yes, London," replied the waitress. "I'd sure like to see that there Buckingham Palace, and Her Majesty. That young queen sure's a pretty lady. It would make my day to see her," she added with a nod of her head. "Watched her coronation. Oh, what a show that was. Ain't got nothin' like that here. All those fancy uniforms and dresses. That was one mighty big party." She smiled at Kathleen.

"I'll be right back with your coffee and tea."

Jerome's mother was smiling. "I love the openness of the people here. They're so friendly. Back home a waitress just takes your order. No conversation. Here, they express their feelings. I love it."

The waitress was soon back with tea and coffee. She stood by Kathleen, and looked down at the baby.

"Oh, isn't she just a darling," said the waitress bending down to take a closer look at Frances. "She's one cute little baby." Then looking at Jerome's mother, she said, "You must be grandma?"

"Yes," replied Kathleen with a smile. "First time."

"Well congratulations, and to mother. Must be your first?"

"Yes." Francine smiled at the waitress.

"Well now, grandma, what would you like?"

Kathleen looked up, and smiled.

"I think my son is going to order for us."

"Well, that's nice of him. I hope he's paying, too." She laughed loudly.

"Everyone's having chicken-in-a-basket with fries."

"Well now, that's easy." The waitress returned to the kitchen.

Ten minutes later she was back with their orders, and the four of them began enjoying tender, succulent chicken, and thin, stubby fries. Jerome's father broke the silence.

"Well, it may not be the Lakeside Bistro, but the food is good. I particularly like the fries with a little Ketchup, as you call it."

"How about the chicken, dad?" asked Jerome.

"Delicious,"

Shortly into the drive home, there was silence in the back seat. Francine looked round to see her in-laws sleeping soundly, their heads touching. It had been a full day for them.

Something Jerome's mother enjoyed was spending time with her daughter-in-law. This she did on a number of occasions during her visit. Francine drove into downtown Seattle with Kathleen, and the two of them window- shopped, and strolled through department stores. Kathleen particularly liked Nordstroms. They stopped for coffee breaks, and enjoyed long conversations over leisurely lunches. It seems that mothers, daughters, and daughters-in-law monopolize what is a prerogative of the female gender, an expertise in analyzing human relationships. Kathleen Callaghan had as clear an understanding of her husband as Francine did of Jerome.

"Two or three days before you arrived," began Francine, "Jerome and I sat on the patio talking. He was discussing his work. He's already introduced three new policies that incorporate mutual funds. They are proving very popular. He worked so hard on these policies. I congratulated him, and told him this was a great achievement for one so new to the insurance business. I remember talking with one representative, who said to me, ' Mrs Callaghan, your husband has a better understanding of the insurance business than most representatives I know. For a young man, that's truly amazing.' Then he added with a big smile, 'But oh, he's a bright young fella. He'll go places.' He's so driven, so ambitious, and he has all the ability to fulfill his ambitions."

"Francine, don't I know it. It was the same with his studies, and with the piano. I remember him saying, ' Mum, I'm going to win a scholarship to Cambridge, and I'm going to be the youngest F.R.S.M in England. A boy from a council house in Eldon, whose father is a bus driver, is going to do that.' And he did, and he will go on achieving."

"But mum, that's what I fear. That night I said to him, Jerome, darling, please don't make me a young widow. He was silent for a moment, then he said, ' Francine, I would never do that.' Promise me then, that you won't make your work your top priority. 'What makes you think I will?' he asked. Because, I replied, I know how driven you can be to succeed, to achieve. ' I suppose I am,' he replied. 'I've always been like that. Maybe now I'll begin to ease up.' Please do, my dear. You also have a daughter to consider now. Then he got up, and came over and hugged me. 'You're right,' he said. ' I have to be less self-centered.'

"I'm glad you did that, Francine. Jerome needs reining in," said Kathleen. "Come on, dear. Lets do a little more shopping." She smiled mischievously at Francine.

One of the last places Jerome took his parents before their departure was the picturesque Olympic Peninsular. Jerome's father stood on Hurricane Ridge, and looked toward the snowcapped mountains, and marveled at the rugged beauty.

"You surely picked a beautiful place to live, Jerome. If only I were younger." There was a touch of melancholy in his voice.

"Would you consider living here, dad?"

"It's too late now, Jerome, to uproot."

"We have so much room. You could always stay with us."

"Not a good idea. There comes a time when children leave home, and make it on their own. They have their own lives to live without parents interfering. Stay in touch, of course, but stay out of their homes. There's also the matter of our friends. They're an important part of one's life."

"Yes, you're right dad. I hadn't considered those points. The wisdom of parents."

"Is that what it is?" said James with a chuckle.

"What I will say though, is you made the right choice," and putting an arm around Jerome's shoulder, he walked toward the large log lodge.

Two days later there was another emotionally wrenching goodbye. Jerome's parents had so enjoyed their visit. For three weeks they had shared in Jerome's initial successes, and all his achievements had amazed them. Kathleen Callaghan had a deeper appreciation of her daughter-in-law. Jerome was in good hands. Francine would ensure that Jerome's ambitions would not rule him. There was in her love for Jerome a sense of agape.

A week after the departure of Jerome's parents, Francine's parents arrived. The weather in mid-August was still warm, though there were some early signs of fall. Like the Callaghans, the Van Dykes fell in love with the house and property, but most of all with Frances, their first grandchild. Lucia held the little child in her arms.

"She's so adorable, and so beautiful. I'll want to take her with me."

"Not at your age mum, no matter how adorable she is."

Lucia laughed. "You're so right. They're a lot of work, and just think, Jerome's mother had three. But let me hold her a little longer," and she gently stroked Frances' head.

Lucia was particularly impressed with the flowerbed Francine had dedicated to her. Herbaceous plants surrounded tall hibiscus with large flowers, and chrysanthemums of different colors. Lucia walked the circumference slowly, deriving pleasure from the assortment and colours of the flowers.

"My dear Francine, this is so beautiful," and stretching out her arms, she added, "They both are. What a lovely tribute to your mothers." She put her arms around her daughter and held her close. "Thank you my dear Francine. I'm sure Kathleen was thrilled."

"She was. Each day, she would walk around both the flowerbeds, and admire the display. I was saddened knowing she would not go back to her own garden."

"She's a lovely lady," said Lucia.

"She is mum. We got to know each other so much more during her visit."

"Ah, mother and daughter-in-law having deep conversation, that's good. Do you think I can do the same with my son-in-law?" Lucia smiled impishly at her daughter.

"Try him mum. I think you'll find Jerome will respond."

"But first I want to hear him play a little Beethoven. Has he been playing?"

"Oh almost every day. Sometimes over weekends he'll practice a piece for two hours. I love it when he does, because I know he wants to stay close to his music."

"He's so talented. He must never stop playing." Francine's mother was serious.

"Jerome will never do that," Francine replied reassuringly.

That evening Jerome played, and Francine's mother listened, eyes closed, a soft smile upon her lips.

Lucia proved to be a poor sailor, but Jerome still took his in-laws to the Lakeside Bistro. Inside, Francine introduced her parents to Mario.

"And mother, Mario loves to flatter the ladies."

Mario looked admiringly at Francine's mother.

"Mrs. Van Dyke, it is the custom of us Greek men to compliment ladies, and perhaps make their hearts beat a little quicker," said a smiling Mario.

"Permit me to say madam, but I see where your daughter gets her beauty." He laughed, and winked at Francine.

"Mario, you're incorrigible," said Francine.

"My dear," said her mother, "I think he's rather charming."

"Mum, Mario does not need flattery."

"Why, thank you Mrs. Van Dyke. Now, may I bring you a glass of wine?"

As Jerome had anticipated, lunch was a pleasant, social occasion. Francine's mother had a talent for putting people at ease, and eliciting pithy conversation. When lunch was over, she had learned more about her talented son-in-law, and she was even more convinced her daughter had chosen well.

To the southeast of Seattle is the snow-capped mass of Mount Rainier. It attracts mountaineers, and would-be mountaineers. Such was not Lucia's interest. She had expressed an interest in having a closer view of this magnificent peak. Jerome was happy to oblige, and on a clear, sunny Wednesday drove Francine and her parents to the lodge situated some five thousand feet above sea level. The last of the alpine flowers were fading, but still made one aware of the beauty that flourishes at even this altitude.

"The air is thinner," said Julian. "I'm gasping already. People climb this?"

"They do dad," replied Jerome. "I wouldn't mind trying one day."

That remark received a dissenting look from Francine.

"Stick with the piano darling. It's much safer," and putting her arm through his, guided him toward the lodge. Frances was asleep in the carrycot.

Lucia looked up at the vast, snow-covered slopes toward Muir Ridge. It was all so different from Singapore's mostly flat, lush vegetation, she thought, and breathed the thin air a little more deeply as she walked toward the lodge.

There were other days like this one, when Francine's parents enjoyed the spectacular natural beauty of Washington State. Indeed, the more they saw of it, the more Julian and Lucia realized their daughter would never return to Singapore. She was in love not only with a remarkable young man, but also with the natural beauty of a remarkable land. Together, the four of them enjoyed wonderful days. Lucia and Julian returned home with cherished memories of their initial visit to America, and their daughter's new home.

End Part IV.

Part V

The Best of England

J ermaine Catherine Callaghan was born on March 11th 1958, almost two years after her sister, Frances. She was not as long, or as heavy as Frances was at birth, but she had the same dark hair and eyes. Both James Callaghan and Julian Van Dyke would have liked a son, but such was not to be. They were happy with two healthy granddaughters. As neither Jerome nor Francine wanted to travel far with a baby, it was not until Jermaine was three that they visited Jerome's parents. Francine's parents had visited a second time in May 1959, and Jerome had paid for his parents to visit again a year later. Now, in September 1961, Frances and Jermaine, ages five and three respectively, were in England for the first time. It was all very exciting.

Jerome wanted to show Francine and his parents the unspoiled counties of Devon and Cornwall. At age sixteen, he had cycled through this part of England, and had fallen in love with it. He wanted them to see the quaint stone cottages in sleepy towns that seemed immune to the changes of a restless, noisy society. Jerome rented a car, and drove his family and parents to that southwest peninsular washed on both sides by the Atlantic.

Their first night in Devon they stopped near Lynton, and stayed at a B and B run by a humorous, loquacious lady, who regaled them with stories about the county. Frances particularly liked her.

"She's funny, daddy. Her tummy jiggles when she laughs," giggled Frances.

The next morning as they were leaving, the lady gave each of the girls a Devon pixie doll. Frances hugged her, though her arms could not encompass the lady's considerable girth.

"Why thank you my dear."

The show of affection was clearly unexpected.

On the way to Tintagel, they visited Clovelly, "the quintessential Devon town," said Jerome. Here, time seemed to have stood still. Even the people moved at their own unhurried pace. Quaint stone houses and stores lined the cobble streets that were for pedestrians only. Jermaine decided that Jerome was going to be her ride down the steep cobble street to the ocean.

"Daddy, put me on your shoulders," she pleaded.

"Okay Smidgen, up you go," and Jerome swept her onto his shoulders.

"Daddy?"

"Yes Jermaine."

"Do little people live in these houses?"

"Well, there maybe some little people do, but there are also people like mummy and daddy live in those houses."

"Oh." Jermaine paused, "They mustn't have very much room."

"You're right sweetheart. Not as much room as you have."

"And they don't have any gardens."

"No, they don't, but you see, they live in such a beautiful little town, they don't need gardens. They do have lovely flower boxes, and they're near the beaches and the sea."

"And there are no cars."

"Right. Isn't that great?"

"Yes daddy. I think I'd like that. I could play on the road. But they have funny stones on the road."

"Yes Smidgen. Those are called cobble stones."

"We don't have any cobble stones."

"No, we don't. This road is very old, and long ago people used cobble stones on their roads."

"Are the cobble stones as old as Grandma and Grandpa?"

"Oh Jermaine, they're much older than Grandma or Grandpa."

"Look daddy, that lady has an ice cream. Can I have one?"

"You're forgetting the magic word."

"Please, daddy, can I?"

"I suppose so, when you ask like that."

Just ahead, Frances heard Jermaine's request. She stopped, and turned around.

"Mum, Jermaine's having an ice cream. Can I have one?"

"May I," said Francine.

"May I what?" Frances responded.

"It's simple, my dear. When you ask for something like an ice cream, or for permission to go out, you always use may."

"Well, may I have an ice cream?"

"Yes dear, you may," answered Francine with a smile.

Soon the children and the grandparents were licking large, creamy ice cream. Jerome's father was smiling.

"Is ice cream only for the young and the old?"

"Too soon after breakfast, and too close to lunch," replied Jerome.

They reached the beach, and the girls ran to the water's edge, and looked for sea- shells. They watched fascinated as the sea swept in, then began to recede rapidly, churning up the sand as it did.

"It's running away, it's running away," Jermaine cried excitedly.

Then suddenly the sea was rushing back, and Jermaine fled, shrieking. Kathleen watched her play, wishing that her granddaughter could always be around, and saddened, knowing that all too soon, Jermaine would be gone, and her sister with her. Jerome walked up to his mother.

"Wishing they could always be near?"

"Yes dear. It's so hard seeing them go. We see them for such a short time. These young years pass so quickly."

"That's my one regret in moving to America. The children are so far away, and you see them so infrequently. I would love for the girls to see more of their grandparents. I hardly knew mine. The one I remember best was dad's father. He was a wonderful man. He died too soon of tuberculosis."

"Talking about dad?" Jerome's father walked up with Jermaine. Her little hand was enclosed in his.

"Yes, he was a good man. Kept me above ground, and I'm so glad he did."

"But mum's mother was always so angry," said Jerome. "In fact, that's all I remember about her. Then she disappeared into a nursing home and died."

"Yes," said Jerome's father slowly. "She felt life had dealt her a poor hand. Why did her favourite daughter have to marry a bus driver, when she should have married a doctor, or an engineer? She never did get over it."

"Sounds like someone I know," said Jerome with a smile.

"Well mum, I think you chose well," said Francine. She had been listening intently to the conversation.

"Thank you dear," replied Kathleen.

"Of course, I agree with you Francine," said Jerome's father with a chuckle.

"You didn't do so badly, James Callaghan," Kathleen replied in her best Irish brogue.

There was a chorus of laughter.

"Why are you laughing Grandma?" asked Jermaine with a perfectly straight face.

"Because your Grandpa thinks I'm funny."

"Sometimes daddy's funny," said Jermaine, as she continued up the cobble street. Then turning to Jerome, she said, "Daddy, put me on your shoulders."

"Do I have to?" said Jerome teasing.

"Yes. I'm tired," replied Jermaine.

With that, Jerome hoisted her on to his shoulders, and she placed her pudgy hands around his head.

On the slow walk up the steep main street, Francine remarked to Jerome, "If you had brought me here before we left for America, I might not have wanted to leave."

"You're kidding, of course," said Jerome.

"Of course. But it is beautiful."

"Yes, it is. I love this part of England. I could almost retire here, but then, I like where we live."

"Yes darling, it's growing on me, too.

"Did I hear retirement?" Jerome's father asked the question.

"Francine was saying how she likes this part of England, and I said I could almost retire here. But we also like where we live. There is the water, as well as the mountains. I think we'll stay put."

"You should," said Jerome's father. "Where you live is so beautiful. You've got everything."

As they drove along the coast road to Tintagel, the site of King Arhtur's castle, and the legendary Round Table, Jerome recited stories of Arthur, and Lancelot, and brave Sir Gawain, who answered the challenge of the Green Knight. Even before they reached Tintagel, Frances imagined a tall knight with blue eyes, and flowing blond hair, astride a great white horse. Walking toward the castle, she looked up at her father, and noted his thick black hair. Well maybe, she thought, her knight would have black hair, and she cosied up to her father.

From Tintagel, Jerome drove south to the picturesque fishing village of Polperro with its stone houses clinging precariously to the hillside. There was about it a charm that captivated Francine. It had an indefinable quality that could not be found in Singapore. For her, England wasn't the damp, bland country she had heard others say it is. But maybe she had seen the best during a time of exceptional weather. There were significant silences during the drive back to Eldon. It was as though everyone was contemplating the farewells that were approaching all too soon. When the time came, Jerome kept them brief. He drove his family to the rental location at Heathrow Airport. For much of the drive there Jerome was silent.

"Something's bothering you, darling," said Francine

"It's dad. I didn't think he looked well. The last two days we were there, he was quieter than usual."

"Yes," answered Francine. "I did notice that about him, but I put it down to our imminent departure. We'd had such a wonderful time as a family. I just thought he was sad at the thought of our departure. He'll miss the girls. He had so much fun with them."

"I hope you're right."

For much of the return flight Francine and the children slept. Jerome did so fitfully. This was Jerome's first return flight to America, and he began to feel good about going home.

End Part V.

Part VI.

INTERLUDE

E ARLY ONE March morning in 1962, Jerome answered the
phone. His Mother was calling. She was crying.
"Jerome, your father has had a mild stroke. He's
presently in hospital, but should be home in two days. Both
Jessica and Peter have been in to see him. Jessica is confident he
will recover."

"Mum, I'll take a flight out tonight. That way, I'll arrive in the
morning," said Jerome.

"I think he's going to be all- right, but I know he'd appreciate
your coming."

"Okay, I'll be there."

"Jerome dear, I'll have Jessica meet you at the airport."

"Thank you mum. I'd appreciate that."

Jessica met Jerome at Heathrow, and he spent a week with
his parents. His father made a remarkable recovery. So much
so, one doctor in the hospital questioned whether or not James
Callaghan had had a stroke.

"Did grandpa have a rest in the hospital?" asked Jermaine.

"Yes he did."

"I think I'd rather rest in my own bed, daddy."

"Well, I think grandpa would too, Smidgen. But this was a special rest."

"Like when ladies go to have a baby?"

"That's right sweetheart."

End Part VI.

Part VII.

REQUIEM FOR A REPENTANT LADY

O NE EVENING at the end of September 1965, Kathleen Callaghan phoned her son, Jerome. She had sad news for him. His father had suffered a second stroke, and was in hospital, in serious condition. Jerome assured his mother he would leave on the next available flight. A quick reference to time differences, and Jerome decided the six o'clock evening flight was a better choice than the morning departure at nine o'clock.

He arrived at London's Heathrow Airport shortly after eleven o'clock in the morning. Jessica was there to meet him.

"Good to see you Jerome, though I'm afraid the occasion isn't."

"It's really bad sis?"

"Yes, I'm afraid so. Too much damage this time. He's in and out of consciousness. I really don't expect dad to last more than two days."

"I've arrived just in time. Poor mum."

"Yes, and you may be fortunate to see him in a conscious state."

Once clear of London, the drive to Eldon was pleasant and relaxing.

"I've always loved this time of year," said Jerome. "John Trethewey used to say, ' This is when God goes wild with His great paint brush.' What a lovely man."

"You miss him, don't you Jerome?"

"Very much. Unrealistically, I just thought he would go on creating beautiful gardens for everyone to enjoy. I was going to invite him to my graduation."

"How are Francine and the children?"

Jessica posed the question deliberately. She didn't want Jerome to get into one of his melancholy moods. He looked at his sister, and smiled.

"They're fine, and they all send their love. In fact, Francine wants to know when you're coming over. Frances is dying to show her doctor auntie where she skis."

"How is their skiing?"

"Amazing. Frances is skiing black runs like a pro, and Jermaine isn't far behind."

"And what about their music studies?"

"Jermaine is good, but Frances is the talented one."

"Like her dad."

"More so. I really think she could make the concert stage, but she's young, and we don't want to push her."

"And will Jermaine continue?"

"Oh yes. I think she'll always play, and enjoy it. She's a very happy child."

"That's so good, Jerome. You're really blessed."

"I know, and I'm so thankful, but how about you? How's your practice?"

"Busy and challenging. I've been turning a few heads in the profession by consulting with two very good naturopathic doctors."

"I think that's commendable. Any romance in your life?"

Jessica blushed slightly. "I was wondering when you were going to ask me that."

"Well my dear, you're not getting any younger, and you know how you love children."

"Actually, I've been seeing a young engineer for the past six months. Paul Lansing."

"Catholic?"

"No. Evangelical and an engineer. How's that for a combination?"

"Wonderful. Francine's been meeting with a group of young women who belong to a growing evangelical church. She calls them ' spiritually refreshing.' So may we expect a wedding invitation soon?"

"Oh Jerome, it's such a big decision. Paul's a good man. Mum loves him. She thinks I should marry him. She's afraid I'm going to end up married to my practice."

"The wisdom of a mother." Jerome smiled. "Has he proposed yet?"

"Yes. Three weeks ago. I said, Give me time. Paul said 'OK, but say, yes.'"

By now they were in Eldon, and Jerome suddenly became quiet. He had mixed feelings when he returned to Eldon. His mother was relieved to see him, and held him close.

"Hello my dear. I'm so glad you're here. Dad so wants to see you, and he hasn't much time left."

She began to cry, and Jerome just held his mother. Then letting go of Jerome, she said, "I must get ready. We should leave soon for the hospital."

∾

James Callaghan lay in his hospital bed, a gaunt looking man, his breathing faint, and shallow. He was conscious, and his eyes brightened when he saw his elder son. Jerome went to his father's bedside, and held his hand. This is a hand that once held me as an infant; this is a hand that once held my child's hand as we walked together; and this is a hand that waved goodbye to me as I left for Singapore, and years later for America. His father began to speak in a voice that was barely audible. Jerome leaned down to hear him.

"You've been a good son, Jerome. I'm so proud of you. Say hello to Francine and the children." Then he looked at Kathleen, and his eyes filled with tears. "Thank you for all the wonderful years together, my darling." His voice was now a whisper, and Kathleen's face was close to his. Then his eyes closed, and his hand slipped from hers. Tears trickled down her cheeks, as she kissed his forehead. James Callaghan, her loving husband of forty-three years, was dead. She felt Jerome's arm around her. She rose from the bed, and let Jerome hold her. Jessica was sobbing, and Peter was looking at his father in disbelief. He had always envisioned his father growing old gracefully, while relishing his grandchildren. With his retirement only five months old, he was dead. Is this what he had worked for? Poor mother. She will not enjoy father's retirement. She will grow old alone. Now Jessica and I will need to stay close to her. Forget America for me, Jerome.

The funeral took place four days later, in the local parish church. While Jerome and Jessica looked after all the business with the funeral home, their mother chose all the readings and the hymns for the service. Father Michael Jardine, the priest who nine years previously had married Jerome and Francine, officiated at the service. He was deeply saddened at the death of James Callaghan. He had anticipated doing a number of different church projects with James in his retirement. Certainly, he had not expected to conduct his funeral service.

Rebecca read James Callaghan's obituary in the local paper, and decided to go to the funeral service. Over three hundred people crammed the small church. James Callaghan was active in his church, and was greatly respected. Rebecca sat near the back, and after the service, remained there until the church was empty. Then she left. Jerome was talking to a small group of people outside. He looked up as she descended the wide steps, and walked toward her.

"Hello Rebecca. Thank you for coming."

"I'm glad I did. Your father was a good man, Jerome, but that didn't surprise me. You're looking well. Obviously you're enjoying America."

"Yes. It's been good to us."

"Enjoying your work?"

"Very much. It's challenging."

"I'm pleased for you, Jerome."

"Thank you."

"And how are you keeping?"

"Oh, I don't know. I live one day at a time." Rebecca's voice was a monotone.

"You've been on your own now for some time."

"Yes. It's eight years since Ronald's death."

"That's a long time. Do you ever think of remarrying?"

"I haven't met anyone, if that's what you mean?"

"I'm sorry to hear that."

"I'm never sure if the men I've been out with are more interested in my money than me. There aren't any genuine men around it seems. So I get more and more involved in the business."

"No horses?"

"No. I haven't ridden in years. Do you have children?"

"Yes. Two daughters, nine and seven."

"You're so fortunate. Are they playing the piano?"

"Of course. Actually, the elder one is more interested in the violin."

"You have no children?"

"No. In seven years of marriage, no children. I have my regrets. And so does mother."

"I can believe that. Incidentally, how is your mother?"

"That is something I mean to tell you. She's very ill. In fact, she's dying of cancer, and wants to see the two of us. I think it's a deathbed confession. She wants to appease a guilty conscience. She wants to make peace with herself."

"I'm sorry to hear about her illness. We never got on, but I wouldn't wish cancer on anyone."

"Can you come over tomorrow morning at ten o'clock?"

"Yes, I can do that."

"Good. Tomorrow then, at ten."

"Before you go, I'd like you to meet my mother."

Kathleen Callaghan, who was talking with a small group of women, turned as Jerome approached.

"Mum, I'd like you to meet Rebecca."

"Hello Rebecca." She took Rebecca's hand. "How thoughtful of you to come. Thank you. I think we were meant to meet a long time ago." She had a faint smile on her lips.

"I think we were, Mrs. Callaghan, but things don't always work out as we hope." Rebecca smiled wistfully at Jerome's mother. "I'm sorry for the loss of your husband."

"Thank you, my dear. Maybe some day we could meet for coffee."

"I'd like that. I'll stay in touch."

Rebecca walked away slowly, and Kathleen Callaghan watched with sadness in her eyes.

Florence Millden sat in a large, comfortable chair, a sick, wizened lady waiting for death. An autumn sunshine filtered through her thinning hair. The cancer had consumed her beauty. She smiled weakly at Jerome, and looked at him with sunken eyes.

"Hello Jerome." She greeted him quietly. "You haven't changed. Still tall and slim, and you have all your thick, black hair. She spoke in a thin, cracked voice.

"Yes, Mrs. Millden, I'm much the same as I was seventeen years ago. A little wiser perhaps."

"Alan tells me you have a lovely lakeside house," she continued, her voice lifting a little.

"Yes. I think it would meet with your approval."

"A little better than your house in Eldon,"

"A little." She just couldn't resist the comparison, and the social dig, Jerome thought.

"Mother," interrupted Rebecca, "you brought us here for a purpose."

"Yes dear, I did. I haven't forgotten. The reason I wanted both of you here is because what I have to say involves both of you."

She paused, wearied from the effort of saying so much. Her breathing was thin and shallow. Tears were forming in her eyes. For a moment, as Jerome looked down at this emaciated woman, he felt compassion. He knew he was about to hear a confession from a very proud woman. Looking at Rebecca, he sensed she knew what was coming.

"You see, Jerome, I'm a dying woman," Mrs. Millden began. "I look at the two of you, and I realize you should be together. You're not, and I'm to blame. I'm the one who stood between you. I'm so very sorry for what I did, and how I lied." She tried to stifle a sob. "Pride, my children. Pride is what did it. I could not see my Rebecca marrying the son of a bus driver living in a council house, so I intercepted your letters to Rebecca, and I burned them. Then I explained to Rebecca why there were no letters. Why you had most probably fallen for the charms of a young native woman; that, after all, you were a young man with strong desires. Rebecca was young; she believed me. But I think you know what happened, don't you?"

"Yes," Jerome nodded. "I knew Rebecca wouldn't ignore my letters."

"How could you have done such a thing?" cried Rebecca angrily. "And you lied to father and me, and you insulted Jerome in explaining why there were no letters. It's too late now, mother. It would have been better had you gone to your grave with your horrible secret."

She began to sob, and Jerome put an arm around her.

"I know, darling," her mother replied weakly. "Oh, I know. I did a terrible wrong to both of you. I knew how much you loved each other," she sobbed.

Jerome looked at her, a pathetic, frail, dying woman. He was torn between compassion and anger.

"From your deathbed you ask for forgiveness," said Jerome. "You've had all these years to think about what you did. It's too late now to undo the wrong you've done. I shall never understand how you could allow your pride to so interfere in the lives of two young people. What use pride now, Mrs. Millden?" Jerome asked a little bitterly. "I feel sorry for you, and at the same time I forgive you, though you committed a terrible wrong against Rebecca and me."

"Oh, I know, I know, Jerome," wailed Mrs. Millden. Then she began to weep uncontrollably.

Jerome saw there was no use staying longer. He took Rebecca's hand, and led her out of the room and into the spacious front hall.

"There is no more to say, is there Rebecca?"

She looked up at Jerome, and nodded silently. He looked at her tear-stained face, and put his arm around her as she cried on his shoulder.

Before long, she looked up. "I've got to stop crying, and you have to go. Thank you for coming. You've been a great comfort."

"Stay strong, Rebecca. You have lots of life to live yet."

"I know dear. It's just that I keep thinking about what could have been," she said sadly.

She opened the door for Jerome, and said a final goodbye. As he walked toward his car, he stopped suddenly, and turned.

"Give my regards to your father, Rebecca. He's a very fine gentleman."

"Thank you, Jerome. I will."

Then Jerome climbed into his car, and drove slowly down the long driveway to the road, recalling a day long ago when he had played the piano for Mrs. Millden for the first time, and walked down this same driveway, angry at the pride of this same dying woman. Rebecca stood watching, sobbing quietly, and grieving over the loss of the one person in her life she had truly loved, and lamenting the loss of a happiness that could have been.

The End.